W9-AWP-919

"They can't be allowed to get away with it!"

Jamie could barely control her outrage. "If we let your father and my uncle manage our lives now, they'll never quit. We'll end up as nothing but store mannequins."

Tom heard her out, leaning against the living-room door. "Have you thought of the alternative? I don't want to lose you, even for a principle."

Jamie shrugged hopelessly. "I love you, Tom, but I still can't do it. Our positions aren't the same. You've been with Malcomb's long enough to assert your authority, to prove you're your own person. I've just arrived. I was bullied into the warehouse, and tricked—"

How could she say that although she'd been given exactly what she wanted, it was important that the decision be hers, not her uncle's?

Books by Dixie McKeone

HARLEQUIN ROMANCE
2642—CONNOISSEUR'S CHOICE
2722—THE MATCHMAKING DEPARTMENT

These books may be available at your local bookseller.

Don't miss any of our special offers. Write to us at the
following address for information on our newest releases.

Harlequin Reader Service
P.O. Box 52040, Phoenix, AZ 85072-2040
Canadian address: P.O. Box 2800, Postal Station A,
5170 Yonge St., Willowdale, Ont. M2N 6J3

The Matchmaking Department

Dixie McKeone

Harlequin Books

TORONTO • NEW YORK • LONDON
AMSTERDAM • PARIS • SYDNEY • HAMBURG
STOCKHOLM • ATHENS • TOKYO • MILAN

Original hardcover edition published in 1985
by Mills & Boon Limited

ISBN 0-373-02722-2

Harlequin Romance first edition October 1985

To the "Dirty Dozen"
who caught most of my mistakes
and helped make the rest.

————————◆•◆————————

Copyright © 1985 by Dixie McKeone.
Philippine copyright 1985. Australian copyright 1985.

All rights reserved. Except for use in any review, the reproduction or utilization
of this work in whole or in part in any form by any electronic, mechanical
or other means, now known or hereafter invented, including xerography,
photocopying and recording, or in any information storage or retrieval system,
is forbidden without the permission of the publisher, Harlequin Enterprises
Limited, 225 Duncan Mill Road, Don Mills, Ontario, Canada M3B 3K9. All the
characters in this book have no existence outside the imagination of the
author and have no relation whatsoever to anyone bearing the same name
or names. They are not even distantly inspired by any individual known
or unknown to the author, and all the incidents are pure invention.

The Harlequin trademarks, consisting of the words HARLEQUIN ROMANCE
and the portrayal of a Harlequin, are trademarks of Harlequin Enterprises
Limited; the portrayal of a Harlequin is registered in the United States Patent
and Trademark Office and in the Canada Trade Marks Office.

Printed in U.S.A.

CHAPTER ONE

'MISS STEVENS, can you get these next? Miss Stevens? *Jamie?*'

Oops, that's me! Jamie Stone, alias Stevens, gave a start of recognition and looked up. She could feel her face flood with the colour of her embarrassment. Resentment at her predicament overrode the other feeling, and she paled, even as the heat of her anger grew. If she didn't have enough to contend with, she was stuck with the phoney name her uncle had given her. If she had time, she would make a list of the reasons why his crazy idea wouldn't work.

But just how was she going to explain to the two receiving clerks that she didn't answer to her name? She thought she had made it clear they were to call her Jamie, but both boys seemed to be shy, and Hugh Belmont had not helped when he put such emphasis on 'Miss Stevens' as he introduced them. They were younger than she was, and at seventeen and eighteen they probably considered her twenty-four ancient. They'd get over their formality in a couple of days, she hoped. All she had to do was live through it.

Carl, the elder of the tow-headed brothers, had turned back to running the automatic belt system that carried the boxes from the receiving platform into the pricing section of the Stone & Stone warehouse. Freddy waited until she had nodded her acknowledgement and went back to work.

Maybe they just thought she hadn't heard them, she thought. Easy enough with all the noise. Anyone could be expected to be a bit rattled and hard of hearing when they were spending their first day in such a madhouse.

As if to give her sagging confidence a boost, Jamie looked around at the confusion. The platform was a beehive of unbelievable activity.

A few hours before, she had shivered at the echoes and the chill of the cavernous area. Its length, more than a hundred and fifty feet, seemed a terrible waste of space. The twenty-foot unbroken expanse of concrete that ran the total length and formed the platform itself dropped abruptly into four large truck bays with ramps angling up to the street level. That morning, she had eyed those four-feet concrete drop-offs with anxiety. Her first thought was to speak to her uncle about putting railings around the potential danger.

Only minutes after the giant doors had rolled up, she stopped worrying about an inadvertent step off the platform. With a roar, the huge diesel trucks backed in, their cargo beds making temporary extensions to the platform. The platform filled with cartons of every size and shape. Drivers vied for her attention as she ran from shipment to shipment, trying to inspect, record them, and sign the receipts. In the meantime she dodged other drivers who unloaded their trucks with handcarts, ran for the continually shrilling phone and kept out of the way of Carl and Freddy.

There were usually six trucks backed up to the platform, with six impatient drivers, the two brothers who were always ahead of her, and she had no idea how many buyers called about their orders. There was only one of her, and she was definitely outnumbered. She had no idea there were so many freight companies, or that they all delivered to the warehouse on Monday morning.

The soles of her feet, clad in tennis shoes, were stinging from the constant standing on the concrete. She had pulled a muscle in her shoulder trying to move a large carton to find the stencilled department number.

Her hair that she had prudently caught back with two ponytail bands was working free. If she just had time for an aspirin to ease her headache, maybe she could ignore the noise, she thought.

Candlemints.

She read the invoice a second time and frowned at the shipment. Somewhere in that pile of thirty-seven cartons was a weirdo. Either she was searching for scented candles or long skinny candy. And the carton would give no indication of the shape of the contents.

Ignoring her aching shoulder, she pushed aside a heavy carton and spotted a box of—spices? Department fifteen. She flipped through the sheets on her clipboard to find her list of department numbers and names. Fifteen was the gourmet kitchen, special supplies and utensils. Spices—condiments. Close enough. Outside she could hear the blaring air horns and huge engines revving with impatience. The driver waiting for her signature was glaring at her. She didn't look any further.

She handed him his copy and dashed across the platform to the shipment Freddy wanted to load on the automatic belt. She had just started around a stack of cartons when a driver with a handcart seemed to appear out of nowhere. The boxes on the cart were stacked higher than his head and he could not see her. Jamie tried to step back out of his way and tripped over some low cartons. Her clipboard went one way and her pencil another as she abruptly sat on the stack.

The cardboard sides weren't designed to hold her hundred and ten pounds, and she felt herself settle lower as the eight boxes crushed in the middle. Meanwhile, her pencil rolled across the floor and was crushed by another driver's handcart.

This isn't happening to me! her mind wailed. Not since she was a little child had she wanted to kick her feet in frustration, so she resisted the impulse. Instead, she blew a strand of hair out of her face and frowned up at the driver, who seemed to think her accident was a joke.

For a moment she just sat, no matter that she had crushed several boxes of expensive men's suits. Her tired body didn't care that she was creasing several thousand dollars' worth of fine worsted lapels. It enjoyed the rest.

'Hey, Doll-baby, that's not the place to take a coffee break,' the driver grinned, and offered a hand, helping her up.

'Thank you.' Jamie's answer was a little shorter than she meant it to be, but in her first morning on the job, she had been sweetied, darlinged and babied to death.

By and large, the truck drivers were nice guys, she had discovered. Several had been very helpful. Those who delivered to the warehouse regularly had known she was new on the job and were patient.

Part of their attitude towards her was caused by the impression she made, she decided. With her dark brown hair plaited and the braids lying over her shoulders, her small face looked naked, vulnerable, her eyes tended to look over-large, like a child's. Dressed in jeans and a matching jacket, and tennis shoes with socks, she looked years younger than twenty-four. Now she was regretting the thoughts that had made her opt for the little-girl appearance. That morning she had awakened with the idea that a different image would somehow separate her from the woman who would later take her place in the executive offices of the store.

But did I have to look like an adolescent? she was wondering before she had been on the job an hour. In her choice of images, she was giving strength to the idea that she knew nothing and had to be led by the hand. These people who cheerfully gave her instructions, ordering her around with impunity, actually worked for *her.* She was Jamie Stone of Stone & Stone, a multi-million-dollar department store complex, and this warehouse was the smallest and least valuable of her properties.

Not that the store was all hers, or she would not have been on the platform that day, but in the executive offices where she belonged. Only forty per cent of it was hers, inherited from her father at his death a few months before. Another forty per cent belonged to her uncle, George Stone, and he was the one responsible for her being on the windy platform under an assumed name, taking orders from truck drivers and the two other receiving clerks.

The sense of injustice that had filled her since her uncle had insisted on the bargain welled up anew. She didn't *belong* on that platform! All her education was directed towards management. In addition to the six years of college, her father had been training her for her position since she was a child.

As she scrambled for the clipboard she wondered about that education. She'd studied economics, management, cost accounting and every conceivable course to help her in business, but none of them prepared her for walking, carrying a clipboard and writing while she dodged other people and jumped at unexpected noises. Something was definitely lacking in her training. Common sense should have provided a solution, but her mind was being overpowered by the noise and bustle invading the platform. She was used to the peace and quiet of a classroom or the well appointed office in the house in Arizona. That was her mind-set, and she felt helpless in the confusion. Nothing had prepared her for entering the company by the back door, being treated as if she were someone who had walked in off the street, hat in hand.

As long as she could remember, Stone & Stone, one of the two major department stores in the state, had loomed foremost in the family discussions. Her mother had died when she was three, killed in the automobile accident that left her father an invalid. Before she was four they had moved to Arizona because of his health. With only the store and Jamie as his interests, Sam had started grooming her early for the position she would take in the company. Profit and loss, overhead, mark-ups, discounts, and percentages were familiar words to Jamie before she knew their meanings.

After her father's death and a period of adjustment, Jamie had put the house in Arizona up for sale. When she told her Uncle George of her intention to take her place in the company, his attitude both surprised and shocked her.

He was adamant in his objection to her having a place on the board of directors, or any managerial position in the company. The reasoning he gave her, that no one was qualified to give orders until they had learned to take them, left her unmoved at first. His threats to use his influence with the other stockholders and members of the board to keep her out could not be ignored.

Nor, when her anger at him subsided, did she completely discount his reasoning. She kept to herself the hours she spent in a Phoenix department store, watching the sales clerks, trying to put herself in their position as they handled irate and rude customers. Several times she bit her lip and wondered if she would not have told some ill-tempered shopper to take her business else-where. As Jamie Stone of Stone & Stone, she could do it, but the sales clerks, dependent upon their salaries, certainly could not.

Her uncle could have a point, she had decided, then she changed her mind. After all, the courses she had taken in management should have prepared her for dealing with subordinates. But did they? Did they cover that rare occasion when, pressed for time, and only interested in her own concerns, she had been short with a clerk or a waitress? To her shame she had to admit they did not.

Her father had insisted that she have a rudimentary knowledge of law, and after she thought over her uncle's threats, she knew she could fight him in court and probably win her case. But after several days of thinking about those sales girls, she had agreed to his bargain. The last thing she had expected was to end up on the receiving platform of a warehouse!

She hurried into the office and found another pencil. Before she could complete the listing of the order she had crushed, Freddy, one of the two brothers who worked with her, was warning her to check in another shipment. Enough was enough, she thought. She turned back to continue listing the boxes, determined she was going to learn that job in one day. She was tired of being instructed by every Tom, Dick and Harry.

The spring wind, blowing in through the giant doors, caught the corner of the page, lifting it as she listed the last carton. In trying to hold the paper in place she tore several of the perforated sections loose. As they sailed up in the air, she dropped her pencil and chased after them, determined they wouldn't get away. The consecutive numbering on the irritating little scraps would mess up her records if she lost any.

Why, she wondered, had she ever let her uncle bully her into taking this job? Could he keep her out of the company if she really made a push? She doubted it, and before the week was over, she just might make an effort to find out. Hastily setting the clipboard on the edge of the conveyor belt, she scrambled over a stack of cartons waiting to be loaded on that same belt and retrieved her tickets.

They were crumpled and dirty. Jamie frowned down at them, wondering why, when she had taken all her college courses on business, they had never mentioned situations like this. Her dad hadn't brought up the subject either. Obviously she was doing something wrong.

Much more, she thought, as she stood up, and she'd have a face-off with Uncle George this morning. Owning forty per cent of the company certainly entitled her to something more than a place on a windy platform! She marched back to the conveyor belt to pick up her clipboard, but she was too late. The belt, which worked on a programmed relay system, and distributed merchandise through the warehouse, was busy doing its stuff. Her clipboard was making an unexpected journey.

She wanted to turn on Carl and Freddy, telling them that this time the error was theirs, but she could see it would be unfair. They might have started the conveyor system and sent the clipboard on its way, but from where they worked, they could not have seen it around the boxes lined up on the belt.

That's it! she glowered at the cartons moving around the corner, making their way to the pricing section. *I'll march right into Uncle George's office and tell him where to put his warehouse!*

She bit her lip in indecision. How was she going to hold her head up when so far her work record was a stack of little tickets, smudged with erasures, eight crushed cartons of clothing, and a runaway clipboard? At least, she could retrieve the clipboard. The Friday before, she had been shown through the building, so she knew where the belt system travelled.

Squeezing between the wall and the belt frame, she went into the pricing section and looked around. The belt made an abrupt turn on the other side of the wall, rose up an incline until it stood like a bridge, six feet above the floor. It travelled around the eighty by forty-foot room, approximately four feet from the wall—

enough room for a walkway and to allow service, she reasoned.

As she stood watching, two boxes passed, and she observed their progress. Halfway down the room a low buzzer sounded as they approached, and suddenly a metal arm swung out from the outside railing, creating an angled obstruction. With the force of the belt pushing them, they shuttled off the main pathway and down a ramp on to a long stainless steel table. The pricing clerk noted their arrival by pushing them aside while she continued to unpack another box.

She was pricing and hanging men's sports coats in a tall canvas-sided cart that hung from a monorail, though it had wheels and could be rolled about. Jamie knew that the monorail and not the conveyor belt was the complicated part of the system. She had been told the merchandise travelled all over the building and on occasion back again without the need of human labour. She had an idea that her uncle and Hugh Belmont were making a joke about that.

Then, remembering her object in coming into the pricing department, she stood on tiptoe, trying to see the top of the belt and locate her clipboard. While she was searching, a woman dressed in a smock shouted, catching her attention. She was holding up the board.

Jamie worked her way between the supports of the belt and took it, sighing as she saw that several more of the perforated slips had been torn off in its travels.

'Thank you,' said Jamie, turning away, but the woman put a hand on her arm, detaining her. Jamie could not help noticing the uneven lengths of the woman's fingernails. The polish was chipped away at the tips. Jamie was fastidious about her own person, and wanted to draw away from what she considered sloppiness.

'Your first day out on the platform, sweetie?'

Jamie ground her teeth together. Why did everyone

have to call her pet names? Still, saying, 'I prefer to be addressed as Miss Stone, thank you,' was hardly the proper answer in the circumstances. Her bargain with her uncle contained the condition that neither of them would tell anyone who she really was.

'Yes, it is,' she answered as calmly as she could.

The woman volunteered her name, Velma Collins, and Jamie was gratified that she remembered to say Stevens.

'What you need is a break,' said Velma. 'Join the rest of us for lunch, honey. At least you'll meet some of the crazy characters around here. Helps to know who's who.'

Jamie wanted to say no. There was no point in beginning a relationship that could not last. And she certainly could have nothing in common with this woman, who struck her as slightly vulgar. Velma was somewhere between forty and fifty, she guessed, but her bright blonde hair with its cute little bows and butterflies, and the two and a half pounds of make-up she wore, left Jamie unsure of anything about her except here was a woman who was still trying to be a twenty-year-old.

'Come on, honey, believe me, you need a break, and we usually have some fun over at the Grease and Glob.' Velma unfastened the smock to reveal a white ruffled blouse and a pair of black cotton slacks so tight Jamie wondered if she could sit down at all.

Before she could come up with a reasonable excuse, two other girls joined them, another bleached blonde who was far too heavy, though she seemed to be younger than Jamie, and a very pretty brunette with bright blue eyes.

Velma made a casual introduction, adding the information, extracted from Jamie, that she was not only new to the company, but to that part of the country. In the conversation Jamie was given no opportunity to say she had other plans. She found herself caught up in the general exodus from the warehouse.

On the street they dodged around the numerous trucks that appeared to Jamie to be in an insoluble traffic jam. Some were waiting for others to unload and clear the loading docks; others apparently wanted the street cleared so they could get through. The impatient horns had started blowing at eight that morning, and continued all day with hardly a pause. In addition, the roaring of giant diesel engines and the hiss of air-brakes assailed her ears. The odour of carbon monoxide seemed to be embedded into the cobblestones of the old street. Stone & Stone was not the only loading dock receiving or sending out cargo, she noticed.

The name Velma had given the cafeteria was enough to destroy Jamie's appetite, so she was glad to see it was actually called Sarah's. She was additionally relieved by the cleanliness. The sparkling glass and stainless steel counter and the bright moulded plastic tables and chairs were like a shining jewel in the sooty, age-darkened warehouse area.

Several other people, both men and women, converged on the door at the same time. No one pushed, but there was a lot of jockeying for position.

'Hey, come on!' someone behind her shouted. 'Why don't you S. & S. people get out of the way, and let some real workers through?'

Shocked, Jamie looked around, wondering why they were being insulted.

Velma, standing in front of her, tossed her head and answered without turning around. 'At least S. & S. doesn't have *top brass* around to keep us on the job!'

'Mr Malcomb's here to see what makes us such good workers,' her taunter called back. 'Going to make all the other departments just as efficient.'

Jamie picked up her tray, eating utensils and napkin

and moved on. Then she heard a deep voice behind her. 'Just making sure S. & S. doesn't spy out our secrets,' he said.

The deep masculine voice was too well modulated, too casual for the bickering, and Jamie turned to see who had spoken. Iris, the stout blonde who had accompanied them from the pricing section, was directly behind her, but over Iris's head she could see the tall muscular man next in line.

Jamie's first glance was arrested by the eyes. Pale grey, almost silver in the artificial light of the cafeteria, they fascinated her as they gleamed from between the dark fringe of lashes that surrounded them. They were slightly at odds with the deeply tanned face, and the medium brown hair, overlaid with a touch of gold from sunbleaching. She looked into a strong face with sensual lips formed in a half smile. His expression and his casual remarks seemed to fit with his stance as he lounged against the end of the counter, one dark arm resting on the shelf where the trays were stacked. She could see the cords of muscle on his arm, half hidden by the turned-up cuff of his pale blue shirt.

Those light eyes rested on her, lazily assessing her in turn. Suddenly she felt terribly uncomfortable, as if someone was prying deeper into her psyche than she could allow. She turned away quickly and concentrated on the bowl of lettuce and the wide choice of garnishes for a salad. Later she wondered why she had filled her plate with beetroot, the one vegetable she detested.

The argument was still going on over her head.

'There aren't any secrets over there for you to protect,' Velma retorted. 'When Malcomb's can hold their own with S. & S., the news will make the papers!'

A chorus of catcalls met that remark, and since the line had started moving faster, Jamie tried to give her attention to the choice of food. She ignored most of the talk until Velma had led the way to a table in the corner, and they were joined by Iris, Llewellyn, the attractive dark-haired girl, and a young man who was introduced to her as Rick. He let her know right away that he was only working in the warehouse until the fall term started at the local college. She didn't care for his attitude, which was slightly contemptuous of his fellow workers.

'Going to be one of our bright boys,' teased Iris, slapping him on the hand with the back of her spoon. 'Grab him, Llewellyn, before he starts eyeing the college girls!'

Jamie could sense that Iris was just joking, making what she thought was pleasant conversation, though she was tactless. Llewellyn blushed. Was it accidental that Iris had hit on the truth? Rick's reaction was to give just an imperceptible twist to his expression, not enough so he could be accused of frowning, but his distaste was plain enough.

Jamie, who hadn't thought too much of her companions when they had invited her to lunch, felt sorry for the attractive dark-haired girl. In Rick's snobbishness, she saw herself of only a few minutes before when she looked her companions over smugly and decided they weren't her type. Suddenly she didn't admire herself very much for her attitude, and knew it would take very little for her to dislike the handsome young college boy. She made an effort to change the subject of the conversation.

'Is Malcomb's warehouse near here?' she asked, not because she was in any doubt about it, but she was looking for a new subject to ease Llewellyn's embarrassment.

'Why, honey, it's in the same building,' drawled Velma. 'The first thing you have to learn about this town is that, wherever there's an S. & S., from the main store across town to the warehouses here, right out to the branch stores, you'll always find a Malcomb's close by.' Velma's voice raised in volume as she made her explanation, and a retort came from a group of women behind them.

'Yeah, every time Malcomb's moves in and draws the customers, S. & S. mooches in to get their share.'

This was getting to be a little much, Jamie thought. After all, from her knowledge of the history of the company, she knew S. & S. had often led the way in innovations. And after all, that was her company they were disparaging. She had taken all she was going to.

'Or set the standards?' she asked, her voice pitched to carry. 'Is it true that Malcomb's is successful by emulation?'

'Oh-ooh, honey,' Velma cried out, raising her cup as if she were offering a toast. 'You just lay it *on 'em!*'

Jamie, surprised at the vehemence behind her words, thought she had said more than enough. Back into her mind came the memories of her little tickets flying away in the breeze, and her clipboard running away on the conveyor belt. Some great employee she was! If her example set the standards, who knew what might happen?

Apparently a good insult was accepted as a challenge, rather than anger. Until they came up with an answer, they filled time with catcalls, whistles and hoots. Several remarks were thrown back, but over the commotion, Jamie could make out nothing for certain, and she was glad. Fine impression she was going to make if, when she took her place on the board, she was recognised as the chief quipster in what seemed to be a running warehouse fight.

A prickling of her skin made her suddenly aware of someone's attention, and she looked up to see those light grey eyes that had been regarding her in the cafeteria line. He was sitting three tables away with two warehousemen in the blue-grey that was the standard colour for Malcomb's packaging and logos.

Since Malcomb's was Stone & Stone's major competitor, she was aware that he was the sole heir to his company. That alone piqued her interest. The Crown Prince, consorting with the troops, she thought, but admitted he did it well. With no one to obstruct her vision, she could see him better. Her original impression, based on one quick glance, had been of a slight stockiness, but she was mistaken. Seeing him now, she realised he gave an impression of largeness at first glance because of a muscularity that had nothing to do with weight.

The strong muscles that showed in his well shaped neck and wide shoulders gave the impression of a man who had worked hard. His arms, what she could see beyond the turned-back cuffs, were those of a man of strength. That image was continued in the broad chest, the flat stomach and the well formed thighs that strained at the jeans as he lounged back, relaxing in the sturdy metal and plastic chair.

Dropping her eyes to her plate again, she waited a moment before she asked Velma a question. She had assumed that she knew the identity of the man from the remarks, but she wanted to be sure.

'Who is that tall guy—the one in the blue shirt?' With her fork, she indicated the direction of her curiosity.

Velma leaned forward, patting her on the hand, and one of her butterflies jiggled as she shook her head wisely. 'Forget him, sugar—that's Tom Malcomb.'

Jamie's face went pink with Velma's implication that she might be interested. 'I didn't—I wasn't—I just wondered who he was.'

'He's a dream come true,' said Iris, rolling her eyes and smiling before she made a moue. 'But what I dream about him stays a dream,' she sighed.

Jamie didn't answer. Her mind was caught up by those enigmatic looks he had given her. She was right, he was Tom Malcomb. Was he a victim of an attitude like Uncle George's? she wondered. Was he doing his time in the ranks before moving up into the executive offices? If so, he didn't seem too unhappy about it. Out of the corner of her eye she saw him rise and leave the table. There was something sensual in the way he moved with such assurance, she thought.

He joined several men across the room. Before long, judging from the ribald laughter, they were telling jokes. Two of the men Jamie recognised as truck drivers who had unloaded merchandise on the S. & S. platform that morning. She envied Tom Malcomb his easy address— but then she doubted if they called *him* honey and baby.

While she was thinking about him, he turned slightly, and his grey eyes met her brown ones again. She ducked her head and made an effort to finish the strawberry shortcake. In spite of the nickname given the cafeteria, the food was good, and she did justice to her lunch, but the shortcake was just too much to handle.

Interrupting her thoughts were those gazes Tom Malcomb had given her. What was there about them that bothered her so? As Velma had said, there was no hope he was interested in her, if he thought of her as a warehouse clerk. He certainly put himself above having affairs with the hired help, didn't he? So the help was hired by the competing company, wouldn't it still be the same? If he grew accustomed to thinking of her as a warehouse clerk, would she ever get past that idle speculation in his eyes?

Suddenly she saw another reason for not wanting to work on that platform, but the very idea irritated her. She had been trained by her father to be a professional woman, to take her place on the board of directors, to run her business and not let other people interfere in her life. Part of her problem was the loss of her father and a bit of loneliness caused by being in a strange place. Still, her mind had no business going into high-flying loops over Tom Malcomb. He was competition, for heaven's sake! She knew there was a buddy-buddy relationship between the executives of the two companies, but this was a little too much.

She put her fork down with decision.

'Thank you for inviting me,' she said to Velma, 'but I should get back and take over the receiving so the others can have lunch.'

She hurried out of the cafeteria and rushed around a huge truck, a sixteen-wheeler, that was trying to slide its bulk into the bay to unload.

After all, I'm here to work, not to gaze cow-eyed at Tom Malcomb, she told herself. She shook away the little thrill that came with a mental objection. *He started gazing first*, it said.

By telephone, the noise of the trucks was heard fifteen blocks away. As he held the receiver to his ear, George Stone looked up at the walls of the small, sedately elegant room. It was the exclusive inner sanctum of the executive dining room of a major department store chain called Malcomb's. But George had no cause for envy. He was Abel Malcomb's guest in the dark-panelled room every Monday. On Thursday they lunched in George's equally exclusive and equally dark-panelled room in his equally major department store directly across the street.

Theirs had been a long association, dating back from the time their fathers had operated out of small, one-story buildings. As boys, they had taken time out from making deliveries and sweeping out the stock rooms to engage in scuffles in the alley. But years before they had learned the benefits of, if not working together, then at least not cutting each other's throats. During the years they had refined both their friendship and their business relationship until they complemented each other. The result had been success, and both stores branched out until they were spread across the state in most of the newer, better shopping centres.

George, a small spare man whose energy radiated from him like a light, sat back in his chair, holding the phone and listening. Across the table Abel Malcomb leaned forward, straining to hear the conversation. A shock of white leonine hair fell over his deeply tanned forehead, and he brushed it back with a hand as he frowned.

'What's happened?' His grey eyes, obviously akin to those Jamie had admired, narrowed. 'She's quit. I told you she wouldn't stay.'

George Stone ignored him as he listened. Suddenly he gave out with a bark of laughter.

'She sat on *how* many boxes of Hamming-Thomas suits?'

'She'll quit,' groaned Abel. 'She'll hire every shyster lawyer from here to New York, and we'll be up to our ears in trouble!'

George hung up the phone and frowned across the table. 'Will you stop your Doomsday mumbling? She won't quit, she won't sue, and if she did, you wouldn't be in it.'

'It's not going to work,' Abel grumbled, and pushed away a piece of lettuce to search out the last shrimp in his salad. He looked up at George and shrugged.

'Okay, you got her here, and she did show up for work, but I drove by the warehouses this morning. There's a madhouse out there, and she won't stay. Besides, with everyone running around like crazy, she won't meet Tom anyway. That's the only hopeful thing about this crazy scheme.'

George, taking a drink of water, set the tall crystal glass down with a force that sent the liquid sloshing. He glowered at Abel.

'What's this—all of a sudden you don't want to get them together?'

'I didn't say that,' snapped Abel. 'But you can't tell me a warehouse is the ideal place to start a romance. Sweat and dirt and diesel fumes aren't quite the same as candlelight.'

'No,' George sat back, grinning, 'but it's hard to get on a high horse out there. In the warehouse they'll be real people—no phoney hoi-polloi. Besides, there, they'll see each other every day. I tell you, it *will* work. And she's too good-looking for any red-blooded man to miss.'

'There's no chance of that,' Abel answered. 'He asked yesterday if she was starting this week. He's curious about her.'

George halted in the act of buttering a roll. With the bread in his left hand, he waved the butter-covered knife in a half threat. 'You told him?'

'Of course I told him!' Abel looked indignant. 'She's going to be using that other name, how is he supposed to know who she is? Don't worry, he won't say anything, but if we want him to get interested, we better point him in the right direction.'

'Abel,' the butter knife was clean and definitely threatening, 'you didn't tell him what we had in mind?'

'Hell, no! Do you think I'm stupid?' The powerful owner of Malcomb's department stores moved back in his chair. 'And quit pointing that knife at me!'

Obediently, George laid the knife aside and looked thoughtful. 'Maybe you had a good idea there.' His grin came back. 'Yeah, I like it. He needs to know who she is.'

'So does everybody else,' groused Abel. 'Your people

are going to think she was pulling something on them.'

'We'll straighten that out when the time comes,' George said confidently. 'She needs to know what it is to be a worker, and she can't learn that as a Stone. They'd fall all over themselves for her if they knew she was the boss.'

'Then she should have taken a job with another company,' Abel argued.

George frowned and shook his head. 'No. I don't have any control over another company. They might not treat her right.'

Abel, still unconvinced, shook his head. 'She won't stay, and you've got no right to force her. Damn it, George, you can't keep the girl out of the executive offices, not when she owns nearly half the business!'

'Hell, I'm not taking the business away from her! The sooner she can handle the whole place, the better satisfied I'll be. I *want* her on the board, but she's got to know what the business is before she can run it! She's got to know the store is more than the statistics she can quote. But she'll keep her part of the bargain. She's a Stone.'

'That's not saying much if she keeps it like you kept yours.' Abel leaned back, still frowning. 'When she finds out she was manipulated on to that platform, and Hugh Belmont is telling you every move she makes, that's it for you, friend. She'll never trust you again.'

George spread his hands, his grin widening. 'So who wants to be trusted? Just as long as she learns what she needs to know and I keep her away from some playboy who wants nothing but her money. She can hate me the rest of her life if she does what she should.'

'You know, George, these youngsters may not see it the way we do.'

'Trust me,' smiled George.

For the first time Abel smiled. 'Ha!'

When George left the fifth floor of Malcomb's, he ignored the elevators and took the slower route by escalator. As soon as his descent allowed for it, his gaze automatically roamed over the various departments. The sales were doing well.

He left the store, giving the door a proprietorial pat as he stepped out into the cool spring sunshine. If he and Abel could pull off their plans, one day the bustling store behind him, and the equally impressive one across the side street, would be joined together under the same strong management of the third generation. He and Abel were getting on in years. They were both getting tired, but not so tired that they were either of them ready to leave their life's work in the hands of incompetents.

Abel had no worries. Tom had always known he was coming into the store, but after college he had decided to strike out on his own for a bit, working his way around the country and much of the world, filling himself with experience and odd bits of knowledge. At first, neither Abel nor George approved of his leaving to make his own way, but in the year he had been back in the store, Abel found his son's time hadn't been wasted. His grasp of everything from sales to the relay systems in the elevators was proving to be an asset. With one question, Tom could convince a mechanic or a service man, a truck driver or a sales clerk, that he knew, if not all about their jobs, at least enough so that no double-talk was going to work with him. Abel was proud of his son—justifiably, George thought.

Jamie was the odd ingredient. In the face of Abel's negative attitude, George had sounded more positive than he felt. He knew, thanks to her father's untiring efforts to train her, that Jamie came equipped with a brilliant business mind. But what else did she have? He was counting on a real sense of heart beneath the cool, professional poise taught her by her father, but he was hoping, just hoping.

All she had to do was call his bluff. Would she? And if she did and stepped into the authority her shares gave her, how would she treat the employees of the store? Did she fully understand the business showed a profit made for it by the buyers, the clerks, the warehousemen, the delivery men? That it wasn't facts and figures but people working together? Did she understand the misery she could cause them by callous treatment, and the problems the stores would have if their better people became unhappy and went elsewhere? Dissatisfaction had a way of filtering down through management, he knew, and he wanted all his people content.

As if to illustrate his point, Myra Simms crossed the floor and stepped behind the hosiery counter. She was a small blonde who had been born faded, he thought. She was not likely to marry. Last week he had presented her with her fifteen-year service pin. Stone & Stone was her life, and she had the right to expect a pleasant place to live it. So should Joseph, he thought, as he saw the old elevator starter holding the private car for him. Joseph boasted ten more years at Stone & Stone than could George. Three times George had tried to talk the old man into taking his pension, but without success.

George's chin jutted out as he stepped into the elevator.

And that damned girl had better not come into the store with some modern ideas and try to force him out, he thought belligerently.

As he walked along the corridor and turned into his office, suddenly George felt his years, as if he had carried some heavy weight for too long. He was an old man, he told himself, no longer wanting the responsibilities he carried, and afraid to put them down.

CHAPTER TWO

DURING the afternoon the seemingly endless parade of trucks suddenly stopped. The receiving platform that all morning had been stacked with large and small boxes finally cleared. Carl and Freddy scattered sweeping compound and, using wide brooms, began sweeping the smooth concrete floor. Their progress was erratic as they used the big wooden-headed brooms as floor-bound weapons. Laughing, they each seemed to be impeding the other's progress as they attempted to scatter the compound and collected rubbish in the front of the other's broom.

Jamie watched the two young men with a thoughtful frown. She was envious of their energy after the exertions of the morning, and wondered if someone shouldn't tell them they were being paid to work.

But as she watched, she could see they were doing their jobs. Behind them, the platform was as clean as the compound and the brooms could make it. And if they did the job, did it make any difference if they turned it into a game? She shrugged and decided it didn't.

Jamie was enjoying the relative peace and quiet too much to worry about the brothers. For a few minutes at least, she was free to sit in the small cubicle of an office and complete her records at the old, battered desk. She frowned as she entered 'ticket lost' by several of the numerically kept records, but written out neatly, the explanation gave no hint of the runaway clipboard, and the numerous other difficulties she had encountered that day.

She was just finishing when a tall, brown step-van

pulled into the bay. The United Parcel Service delivery always arrived in the afternoon, she had been told. She picked up the clipboard and searched through the papers held in place by the large metal clamp. She had been given special instructions for the UPS shipments, but apparently they had accompanied some of the tickets into the land of the lost.

As Jamie left the office, she cast a worried look around the area. Hugh Belmont, the warehouse manager, was taking a late lunch hour. She stepped into the passage where Carl and Freddy had disappeared, but neither they nor their brooms were in sight. Since no assistance seemed to be available, she was on her own, she decided. With a sigh, she went over to where the UPS driver was stacking small packages on the edge of the platform.

'Afternoon, pretty good load today,' he called as he worked at top speed. Jamie stood watching him, wondering why all the drivers for that particular company always seemed to be on the run. Kneeling, she tried to sort the small parcels, but he kept tossing others on to the pile until she was thoroughly confused.

'Forty-seven,' he said, making a slash down the page, and thrusting it into her hands. 'Just sign here.'

'But I didn't get a chance to count them,' Jamie objected. She took the clipboard he handed her, but made no attempt to affix her signature.

With a long-suffering expression, he jumped up on the platform, quickly piling the boxes in stacks of five— 'Five, ten . . .' in no time at all he had counted out forty-seven boxes, and Jamie, not knowing what else to do, signed the sheet and let him go.

When he drove away she was sitting on one leg, the other hanging over the side of the drop into the bay, trying to get the boxes in an order she could understand. Many of the return addresses she recognised, but some were without any identification of the manufacturer. Five boxes, with the department twenty-one added to the warehouse address, had only a number in the upper right-hand corner.

'Now, what am I supposed to do with them?' she muttered as she tossed one over out of her way. She frowned as the package slid further than she intended. The breeze blowing in the high open doors blew her hair in her face and she pushed it away angrily. Just something else trying to foul her up, she decided, but the breeze was not the major offender. That little box was.

Suits me, I don't want you anyway, she thought, and slid the others after it, watching them ricochet off each other and scatter. She knew she was making a game out of her frustration, but it was hers to do with as she willed.

'Don't throw them out to be stepped on,' ordered a voice behind her.

Jamie slid around to see Tom Malcomb standing over her. The relaxed attitude she had seen in the cafeteria was gone. He stood, his hands on his slim flat hips, glaring down at her as if she was some insect that had crawled into his domain. Those light grey eyes seemed to bore into her with all the haughtiness of the Crown Prince she had mentally tagged him.

If he wants to play the big shot, let him do it in his own area, Jamie thought. Her voice was cold enough to chill half the city. 'I beg your pardon?'

For a frozen moment they stared at each other, only a mutual and active dislike seemed to be alive. She sat, one leg still curled under her, the other drawn up in front of her as she gazed up at him. He, with his legs slightly apart, could have been captaining a ship, she thought, or ordering troops into battle. His attitude seemed too far-reaching, too powerful to be exerted on a warehouse floor. Certainly on *her* warehouse floor.

'If you don't mind, I'll make my own arrangements,'

she said, refusing to be daunted by his demeanour. 'Is there something I can do for you?'

His mouth tightened slightly, those silvery eyes still gleamed like weapons. Then he bent down, carefully picking up the five small packages and placing them in the shelter of a concrete support column.

'The first thing you can do for me is *not* to throw fifty thousand dollars' worth of jewellery out where a forklift might run over it.'

Jamie gritted her teeth and held on to her clipboard with both hands, fearing she just might throw one of the small boxes at him.

'I doubt if your estimate of their value is correct,' she snapped. 'Anyway, it's no concern of yours.' She knew he was wrong—fifty thousand dollars in jewellery would hardly be tossed on a platform floor. She couldn't imagine such a thing.

'I beg *your* pardon,' he threw her own words back at her, giving them the force she had tried for. 'Hugh Belmont didn't turn you loose without a departmental list. Check your department twenty-one and see what it handles.' His curt order heated her blood another ten degrees.

'All in good time,' she replied coolly, determined not to take his orders and afraid to look, because he just might be right. 'Now what can we do for you? I understand it's against the rules for unauthorised people to be on the platform.' That should let him know where he stood with her. 'And we don't have forklifts.' She felt on safe ground, since none had been in use that day.

'But we do, and we put them to work when necessary,' he retorted, pointing to the door at the end of the platform. A forklift was jockeying for the proper alignment to get through the door. 'Just warning you Jake is coming. Part of your Banner's shipment ended up on our platform.'

Jamie knew how a sail felt when it luffed. All her feeling of outrage suddenly escaped. She bit her lip, wondering what she should say next. She took refuge in formality.

'Thank you,' she said, getting to her feet. 'If you'll be so kind as to excuse me, I'll unload it and free your driver.' She strode over into the path of the heavy vehicle, forcing the driver to come to a halt. Not until then did she notice the size of the cartons on the wooden flat. They were enormous!

If I try to pick up one of those, I'll be mashed into the concrete, she thought, but she had told Tom Malcomb she would, and there was nothing for it but to try. She took a deep breath, set her feet and heaved at the top box, which was three feet by three feet by four feet. As she put maximum strength into that effort, it came up suddenly.

The carton was unexpectedly, ridiculously light, and her effort was helped by the stiff breeze that was blowing into the loading bay. She stepped backwards, trying to keep from being thrown off balance by her own force.

Suddenly a pair of strong arms encircled her, keeping her from falling over backwards as she tried to hold on to the carton. The surprises, coming all together, caused her to lose her grip. As the box went tumbling, she was caught in Tom Malcomb's arms. She felt his strength as he kept her from falling, and for a moment she clutched at him, needing that security he was offering. She could feel the muscles of his chest as she leaned against him, the firmness of his thighs as they pressed against her legs, and noticed the subtle scent of an aftershave used sparingly. Then she realised where she was. In Tom Malcomb's arms. Of all the people to come to her aid, he was the last she welcomed!

'What was that?' she demanded as she turned in his arms and selfconsciously pushed away from him.

He let her go without a struggle. But his grin, and the matching expression on the face of the forklift driver, said they enjoyed the joke.

'A box of feathers,' he said, his pale grey eyes reflecting the light of his humour. 'I told you the shipment was from Banner. Hugh may not like your treatment of down pillows.'

First he tried to order her around, then he laughed at her! Jamie wasn't sure which she disliked most. 'I'll be more careful in the future,' she said crisply, but when she turned to pick up the carton, he forestalled her. The joke had apparently broken his earlier mood. His eyes that had been so haughty, his arrogant attitude, had disappeared, and instead she saw a soft humour in the grey eyes, and his smile, slow and enticing, was definitely dangerous to female hearts.

'You don't want to put them on the belt,' he said, picking up the box and putting it back on the truck. 'The conveyor can't handle boxes this size. Let Jake take them around.'

'Well, I don't know,' Jamie faltered, not sure whether what he was suggesting would have the approval of Hugh Belmont. She wished either Carl or Freddy would come back and take over the situation. Nor did she really trust this friendly attitude when he had been so abrupt before.

'Like you said, you don't have a forklift on the platform,' said Tom. 'Just let Jake handle it.'

With the same authority he had been showing since she had encountered him earlier that day, he took her arm and guided her back to the UPS shipment.

'You really shouldn't leave these alone,' he said, picking up the five packages. He dropped them into one of the large plastic cartons that were stacked in the corner.

'I know, fifty thousand dollars' worth of something,'

Jamie said sarcastically. 'We always leave valuables like that lying around on a warehouse floor.'

'They didn't turn you loose without a departmental list.' Tom Malcomb took the clipboard from her hand and flipped through the pages until, near the bottom of the sheaf of papers, he pointed out a list of departments and the merchandise they handled.

Department twenty-one . . . Fine Jewellery.

'Oh,' said Jamie, looking at the listing, back at the five small boxes and then, reluctantly, up at those beautiful grey eyes lashed in black. 'Maybe it *is* fifty thousand,' she murmured.

'Probably not—I have this habit of exaggerating,' he smiled, and his eyes were soft. 'But you never know. The really big shipments usually come by special courier, but a lot of valuable stuff comes in those plain little boxes.'

'But—but that's *crazy!*' Jamie spluttered. 'No protection, no insurance—'

'On the contrary,' Tom replied. 'If, say, you were getting a shipment from Tiffany's, which neither of us does, one look at the box with their name on it, and everyone between New York and here would know what he's handling. In a plain box, who would think there might be several thousand in jewellery—' he picked up another small package, hefted it and handed it to Jamie, who was surprised at the weight. 'Department 59— check, I'll bet it's silver.'

'So, I'll watch it more carefully,' said Jamie, ready to admit when she was at fault, though she didn't like it much.

'Then don't go throwing the stuff around,' he said, once more on the authoritative pedestal that brought her ire up. She straightened her shoulders and met his gaze.

'Thank you for the instruction, but I think I should get back to work.'

'Oh, and list them,' he pointed to the arrival records

she was filling out, 'according to carrier as well as brand name on the box and departments.'

In spite of his help, she was tired of orders, and again she decided she didn't have to take any from him.

'Thank you, sir,' she snapped. 'But if you don't mind, I'll handle it according to the way S. & S. does it. I don't work for you, you know.'

'Honey, you wouldn't,' he said with a smile, and turned away, sauntering back towards the door that led into Malcomb's warehouse.

'Maybe I'd better take back what I said,' came a voice behind Jamie, and she turned to see Velma coming across the floor of the platform. Her gaze was on the retreating back of Tom Malcomb until he disappeared. 'Maybe you've got what it takes to land that guy after all.'

'I hardly think so,' Jamie retorted, and tried to turn back to her list, but Velma shouted for Freddy and took the clipboard out of her hands.

'Dearie, you must have a terrible impression of S. & S. They don't make you work all the time. You do get breaks.' As Freddy came up, Velma handed him the board and he immediately started listing the shipment, faster and more competently, Jamie noticed. But he did have more time on the job, she reasoned.

'Now, you come along with me. We're not completely uncivilised. We've got a little lounge over here—nothing special, but I bet those men forgot to even mention it. Did you even have a cup of coffee at morning break, sweetie? Just come along with me, and I'll show you what's what.'

Jamie meekly followed Velma as she led her back into the recesses of the warehouse to sections she had not been shown. She was glad enough to let the voluble older woman get her a Coke from the machine while she took a seat on a lumpy vinyl sofa. Her muscles were throbbing from pushing around boxes, from bending over to read labels, and a hundred other little moves that were not a part of her normal exercise programme. A few minutes to sit and rest, to moan over the wounds of the day, would be wonderful, she thought. But Velma had something else in mind.

'I'd say, from what I saw, that Tom Malcomb liked you,' Velma commented.

'Oh, you're out there,' Jamie retorted. 'He's just looking for someone else to give orders to.'

Velma's carefully plucked and pencilled eyebrows arched as she smiled wisely.

'Let me tell you something, sugar. When old Velma doesn't recognise a gleam in a man's eye, she'll be dead. Now what we've got to do is get you fixed up so he'll pay more attention to you.'

'No,' Jamie announced positively. 'That's the last thing I want. Thank you, but no. I am not interested in Tom Malcomb.'

What she said to Velma, she intended to be the truth. She had too much to do to think about him. He was not going to intrude in her thoughts—so why did she still feel those strong arms around her as if he had not turned her loose, and why did those light, laughing eyes seem to be everywhere she looked? I'm not interested, she told herself, and knew she was lying.

George Stone pushed back his coffee and leaned back in his chair, staring over the stemmed glassware at Abel Malcomb. It was Tuesday, and they were in the small, dark-panelled dining room of S. & S. Abel, told by his doctor to cut calories, was picking at a salad, obviously dissatisfied.

George broke the silence. 'Do you have an extra forklift?'

'How the hell do I know? I don't carry an inventory in

my head,' Abel answered morosely, staring balefully at the half-eaten slice of coconut cream pie George had pushed away.

'Well, I need a forklift, and I don't have one to spare,' George answered. 'I'll never hear the end of it if I don't find one.'

Since when do you head up the supply department?' Abel grumbled, still eyeing the pie.

'Since Jamie has decided she wants one. Tom has one, and what Malcomb's has she thinks S. & S. should have. One day on the job and she starts turning things around! I'm beginning to wish she had stayed in Arizona.'

'So does Tom,' chuckled Abel. 'The argument yesterday shows he noticed her.'

'Yeah,' George grinned. 'At least they won't ignore each other—no, you can't have that pie, so keep your hands to yourself.'

Abel looked indignant. 'Then keep it. Malcomb's makes better pie anyway.'

George glared across the table. 'Not coconut!'

'But you've never been able to touch our pecan,' said Abel, getting to his feet.

'You got pecan today?' George frowned a moment and threw his napkin down. 'Wait a minute, I'll come with you.'

Enough was enough, Jamie thought as she ground on the starter of the old Volkswagen. She didn't mind the small apartment her uncle had found for her. Taking care of it herself would be fun, and now, with a kitchen to herself, and no cook to claim it as private domain, she found she liked cooking and was good at it. Trading her designer-labelled clothes for less expensive ones was unimportant, but an old car that refused to start was carrying the role-playing too far.

She sat in the parking lot and stared out at the rain. She had stayed on the platform a little later than necessary, but a larger than usual number of shipments had kept them busy all day. She was late finishing her records. Most of the others had left on time, so she was sitting in the almost empty lot alone.

And where should she go for help? she wondered. The warehouse was locked, and since she was still unknown to the security guards, she doubted that they would let her back in the building to use the phone.

The other buildings in the vicinity looked equally dark and bleak. The main store was fifteen blocks away, too distant to enlist the help of her uncle. And they had agreed she should stay out of his office.

But where did she go for help? If she could push the car and get it moving, she could get out on the street and roll down the hill for blocks. But would she find a service station along the way?

And if she found none, would she be any worse off than she was? Once the car was moving, it would be more comfortable to steer it than to walk in the rain, she decided, and certainly there was no help available where she was.

After trying the starter one more time, she gave a sigh, fastened her jacket and tied a scarf over her hair. She checked to make sure the emergency brake was off and the car in neutral before she stepped out into the rain.

'Let's see, keep the door open,' she muttered, glad she had backed into the parking space that morning. 'Turn the wheel, so we'll be pointing at the driveway, and be ready to jump in when there's speed—'

'Here, before you get too industrious, let me take a look at it.'

Jamie looked around to see Tom Malcomb crossing the parking lot. This is a little too much togetherness, she thought, then remembered the parking lot was not the property of either store, but one of a chain where the driver paid a monthly rate. It was also the nearest to the warehouses. But even if she still rankled over his authoritative attitude of the day before, she was glad to have help with the car.

'I think the battery is gone,' she said.

Rather than take her word for it, Tom slid into the seat and turned the key. The starter groaned weakly for a second before he turned off the ignition.

'Battery's gone,' he said, frowning at the steering wheel.

Jamie felt like saying she had told him that, but this was no time for making enemies. She didn't know the neighbourhood well enough to know where to find a phone to call a taxi, or where to catch a bus.

'We can push it and get it started, but you'll still have to get a battery,' Tom said thoughtfully.

'If we got it started couldn't I drive it to a store?' Jamie was suddenly reluctant to drive it anywhere. She disliked the willing dependency welling up in her, but in the face of his competence, she wanted to leave the entire matter in his capable hands.

That was Jamie Stevens, not Jamie Stone, she decided. A Stone did for herself, and a Stone would remember that hateful, arrogant attitude she had seen in him the day before. Then she sighed and forgot it. Jamie Stevens had worked all day, she was tired, hungry and chilled by the rain.

Tom shook his head. 'It means a lot of cross-town driving, and it might stall in traffic—does it usually stall?'

'I don't know; I only bought it three days ago,' Jamie explained. 'It's been behaving fine until tonight.'

'Where do you live?'

She told him, and he nodded, satisfied. 'The best thing, I think, would be to take it to your place. Then I'll drive over and get you a battery. It's nothing to replace.'

'In the rain?' asked Jamie, thinking he could get electrocuted.

'It's not raining inside the car,' Tom pointed out. 'Your battery is under the back seat, not the hood.'

'But that's too much,' she objected. She had only met the man the day before. She had no right to put him to such trouble, but he gave her no more time to argue. He pulled a set of keys from his pocket and pointed to a Jaguar parked three spaces away.

'You drive mine, and follow me. I'll take yours, in case it stalls and has to be pushed again.'

Jamie still wanted to object, but he was out of the car and pushing it across the lot. With his strength, and the gradient to aid him, he was soon trotting along beside it before he jumped in. By the time Jamie had opened the door of the Jaguar and started the engine, the Volkswagen had stopped, but she could see by the vapour coming from the tailpipes that he had managed to start the Volkswagen's engine.

When she was ready to turn out of the parking lot, Tom led the way, taking her by the back streets so that they stayed out of the heavy traffic. After Jamie had tested the brakes, familiarised herself with the gears and had adjusted her touch to the gas pedal, she leaned back against the upholstered seat and relaxed. She appreciated a luxury automobile, and the one she was driving certainly fitted that description. She made a critical survey of the inside and decided the car wasn't new. A few telltale scratches on the dashboard, pocks on the windshield where it had been nicked by flying rocks or gravel, and the worn front mats on the floor by the brake and gas pedal, testified to some use.

The leather seat had conformed to a larger frame than hers, and it seemed as if she could feel the presence of Tom Malcomb, as it contoured around her. Along with the smell of leather, she could also detect another scent—she recognised the shaving lotion he wore. Funny, she thought, she had noticed it the day before, and it must have stayed in her memory. Too much of that man was staying with her, she told herself, but not too firmly. After all, he was certainly giving her the help she needed.

When they drew up in front of the picturesque old Spanish-style apartment buildings, Tom parked the Volkswagen and came over to open the door for her.

'If you'll let me use your phone I'll see where I can locate a battery tonight,' he said.

'But that's asking too much—'

'Not unless we're going to argue about it until nine o'clock. Then the stores close,' he countered. 'Now come on, do you want to drive that car tomorrow, or have you made arrangements with a chauffeur?' His insistence on handling the situation was softened by that special smile. It said, relax, trust me, let me handle it. It gave its orders wrapped in silk, and she obeyed its caress.

Thanking him again, she led him into the building and opened the door of her apartment.

She flipped on the light and looked around. Then she remembered she had planned to be careful who she invited in. The large complex in which she lived was picturesque and the rooms were large, but the buildings were old, and the rent was affordable for someone on her present salary. The furnishings definitely weren't. Her uncle had offered to fit out the apartment for her, but at the last minute she had rebelled. The furniture she inherited from her father was both valuable and beautiful. But more important, each piece was upholstered with her memories. She couldn't bear to leave anything behind.

The apartment, though reasonably large, would hold very few of her possessions, but part of the living room set was there. Only the china closet, table—without leaves, and six of the chairs could be fitted into the dining room, but their quality could not be hidden. Nor would anyone believe the sparkling hand-cut crystal and the china on display had come out of a discount store.

Then she nearly choked. Lying on the sofa was her sable jacket. She had intended to put it into fur storage that morning, but was late and had forgotten it. Now there it lay, and even if he accepted some tale about the furniture, Tom would be smart enough to know the fictitious elderly relative she was dreaming up wouldn't have left her that.

But wonder of wonders, he hadn't noticed it. He showed more interest in checking the view from her windows. Jamie hurried to the sofa. What could she do with the jacket? In desperation she dropped her light coat over it, leaving the two garments spread out, taking up half the sofa. She just hoped Tom wouldn't want to hang around.

She was standing by the coffee table, her face innocent of any duplicity, when he turned.

It was too much to hope that Tom Malcomb, used to merchandise and its cost, would be oblivious to what he saw.

'Nice,' he said, his eyebrows going up, his eyes full of laughter.

Jamie waved her hand with a nonchalance she didn't feel. 'I'm indebted to an elderly aunt for the furnishings,' she said casually, though inside she cringed. She could just imagine what he thought. No one on her salary could afford to live as she did. He could be thinking anything, even that there was probably a sugar-daddy in the background paying the bills. She half expected him to tell her to call her mythical benefactor and have him replace the battery, but he didn't.

He glanced around and pointed down the hall. 'Phone down there?' he asked.

'Yes, but maybe the one in the kitchen would be more convenient,' said Jamie. Helpful or not, she would rather he stayed out of her bedroom, but he ignored her suggestion. He turned into the short hallway, and moments later she heard the door softly but firmly close.

Is he breaking a date? she wondered. He certainly didn't need privacy to call an auto supply store. Not knowing what else to do, she stood waiting in the living room until he came back.

'I can pick up a battery not too far from here, so we can have you operating in an hour,' he told her. 'Nothing to putting it in, once we have it.'

'That's too much trouble—' Jamie tried to object again. Seeing his face close, she gave up her hesitancy to accept his help. 'I'm certainly in your debt—' she let the words hang, not sure where to go from there.

'Then repay it,' he said promptly. 'By the time I get that battery and put it in, I'm going to be hungry. That's a good-looking kitchen,' he jerked his head in the general direction of the one modern room in the apartment. 'Can you do anything in it?'

'That I can do,' Jamie answered, smiling. 'If I find anything edible, that is.'

As she closed the front door after him, she leaned against it, staring across the room at nothing. It had suddenly occurred to her that she was encountering a first in her life. She had never had a dinner guest when she had been responsible for the meal; the instructions in Arizona had been passed along to the cook. The delicious odours coming from the kitchen had prompted Tom's suggestion that he would be hungry, she knew. Still, she had a lot to do. She wanted everything to be perfect.

Because it's the first dinner I've ever served anyone, she told herself, resolutely ignoring the fact that her guest was Tom Malcomb.

In the kitchen she leaned over the counter to peer into the top of the crockpot, though she could see nothing because of the condensation on the lid. Inside, a small beef roast, potatoes, onions and carrots had been steaming away all day. To Jamie there was something a little mysterious about putting everything into the cooker in the morning and finding it all prepared when she came home from work. Uncle George had given her the cooker as a housewarming present when she moved into her apartment, and in desperation she had used it because she needed her time to get settled. The results had been excellent, so she gave its warm side a pat and went to grab a quick shower while Tom was out getting the battery.

He had said an hour, which might, she thought, mean an hour at most. Hurriedly she finished her toilet, and hesitated only when she opened her closet. Several of her dressier dresses looked inviting, particularly a deep rose silk that did wonders for her hair and complexion, but she pushed it aside. No slinkies, she decided. Better to stay with slacks and a shirt. Let's not give him the idea he's entered a man-trap.

The last thing she needed was a man entering her life—even a man like Tom Malcomb, but her eye kept straying to the rose silk. Would it hurt anything for him to see she could look good once in a while? Yes, if he thought she had dressed just for him. Should she be just a little daunting, in one of her severely cut business suits, with her hair up in a bun, and her glasses on? No, that hardly projected the image of a girl who worked on a warehouse platform. She resolutely closed the door to the closet.

She was right to hurry. With a little time out to brush her hair and put on lipstick, she hurried back to the kitchen, and had just finished tossing a salad when the door bell rang. She opened it to admit Tom.

In the light over her apartment door, he looked all aglitter with the raindrops sparkling in his hair and on the waterproof jacket he wore. One strand of hair had fallen across his forehead, giving him a little-boy look, which was enhanced by his stance as he stood with his hands behind his back. The way he was standing brought out a curiosity in Jamie. When he had stepped in, she moved sideways to see if he was holding anything.

'What are you hiding?' she asked.

At that he brought his hands in sight, empty but soiled. He dutifully pointed out and enumerated the smudges on his right hand. 'Dirt. A little grease—I think that's a pencil mark—'

Jamie laughed. 'Away to the soap and water with you, while I set the table.'

When he walked into the dining room he cast an appreciative eye over the room. The mirror finish of the dark table had been hidden under a sparkling white tablecloth. The china, plain white with wide bands of wine and gold, was set off by the almost metallic gold of the curtains and the deep colour of the burgundy Jamie had poured into a decanter. Not sure if she wanted to give the room a romantic atmosphere, she had not lit the tall wine-coloured candles in their crystal holders. But when she returned from the kitchen with the large salad bowl, they were burning. The overhead light was off, and one of the lamps on a side table was lit.

'Fancy atmosphere for a crockpot dinner,' she said flippantly. Inside her heart was beating until she wondered if he would hear it. She was half regretting her invitation, though it had been hardly that, since Tom had practically invited himself.

Not only had he issued the invitation, but he was taking over, as he did the serving. When Jamie felt a slight resentment rise that he could make himself so at home, she reminded herself that he was used to taking over. She shouldn't think anything about it. After all, he considered her to be one of the employees who, if she worked for him, would be expected to take his orders and leave him to boss things. But in their private lives? she wondered. Oh, stop worrying about it and eat your dinner, she chided herself.

Crockpot had outdone itself. The roast and vegetables were perfect. Her salad was crisp, and the wine was superb.

Jamie had worried about the candles giving Tom romantic notions, but the one-sided conversation during dinner was on the subject of the warehouses. Had she been any other female, she would have been bored, but since she expected the store to be her life, she had no objections.

He spent nearly half an hour explaining that very few department stores had had the foresight to buy up warehouses in the less expensive part of town, but both Malcomb's and S. & S. had foreseen rising property values. They had both put their receiving departments, large item storage and repair shops in a district where rents and taxes were lower. As a result, the high-priced property in the centre of the business district and in the shopping centres was kept for the business of selling.

'Keeping the unpacking, checking, and pricing on an assembly line basis,' Jamie murmured.

Tom's light eyes glittered in the candlelight. 'Sounds as if you've been doing some thinking.'

Watch it, Jamie gave herself a warning. She wasn't supposed to give away her cover, as Uncle George had called it, but how was she supposed to pretend she had no brains at all? That wasn't going to work, she was sure to give herself away. She folded her napkin and laid it by her plate.

'It just stands to reason that if you take a person, give them a job, and leave them to do it, they'll be more efficient than the person who has to skip from one thing to another—like a sales clerk who sells, unpacks, prices, and tries to keep up with stock on hand.'

'So you know your way around the business,' he commented. Did she catch a teasing tone?

She thought fast. 'Oh, I did a little clerking in Toledo, Ohio,' she lied with what she hoped was aplomb.

'Johnson's? Frederick's?'

Jamie forced a smile. 'No place so grand—just a little discount store.'

What had caused that gleam of laughter in those light eyes? Had she said something wrong? Didn't Ohio have discount stores? Maybe there was a law or something.

She wanted to kick Uncle George! What was Jamie Stevens' background? Was she supposed to make it up as she went along? What else could she do? Her father had taught Jamie Stone to keep a poker face, but somehow that training didn't seem to be a part of Jamie Stevens' background.

When they finished dinner, Tom insisted on helping her to clear the table. In the kitchen, he put the dishes in the dishwasher while she arranged a coffee tray. While she arranged the cups, the coffee, cream and sugar, she gave herself an order with each placed item. She would be careful what she said, she would play the store clerk, and not even think of anything else.

She decided she had been on the brink of too many disasters, and there weren't going to be any more. But as she followed Tom into the living room as he carried the tray, she realised she had set herself up for one. She had forgotten that damn jacket!

Tom, reaching the centre of the couch, paused, looking down at the light raincoat Jamie had carefully spread over the offending article. He was waiting for her to remove them, she knew, but no way was she going to touch that coat. She had brushed through just fine up until now, they could sit on the other end of the couch. Not knowing how to explain it, she reached out and pushed at his back, urging him forward.

He put the tray down on the coffee table and before he could sit down, Jamie slid on to the sofa, forcing him into the corner as she stayed away from the coats.

He looked slightly surprised, but her smile of triumph, too powerful to be hidden, suddenly froze. She realised how the scene must appear to someone who didn't know she had a reason for not moving those coats. To her left, two of the four seat cushions were not being used, seemingly to no purpose. She had forced Tom into the end cushion, and was sitting far closer to him than appeared necessary.

What was he going to think? What else—that she was making a play for him. Her eyes darted about the room, wondering how she could get out of her newest mess. With trembling hands she poured the coffee, handing him his cup.

Tom accepted his cup and put it on the low table in front of him. Then he turned slightly, his fingers just touching the side of a Ming bowl that sat on the end table beside him.

'Your uncle had nice taste.'

'Yes, he always did,' Jamie answered automatically, and when the realisation hit her she almost dropped her cup. She had told him the furnishings came from an aunt, hadn't she? Or did she? Either she had to get out of this mess or develop a better memory.

And what was that startled look on his face just after he asked the question? The words had just left his lips when he looked as if he could have bitten them back.

She felt like saying, 'Hey, *I'm* the one pulling the

scam!' but her narrow escape was enough to keep her mouth closed.

Tom drained his cup. He reached for the pot and poured more, then sat back, sipping at it.

What am I going to do? Jamie wondered about her predicament. What if she got up and moved? She would create awkwardness, and feel foolish. After all, he was busy with his coffee, maybe he had not interpreted her actions the way she had thought he would. Then, if she ran like a scared rabbit, he'd have a good laugh at her expense. He'd laugh even harder if he thought she had attempted to manoeuvre him and then lost her nerve. No, she'd stay where she was and hold her own.

She held the cup and saucer, trying not to feel like a teenager on a first date. Not that she had ever had that many dates, she thought, suddenly realising her inexperience. Her life had been full of study, helping to look after her father, and working with him as he constantly pored over the business records and wrote voluminous letters to his brother at the store. Sam Stone had been proud of his daughter's grasp of the business, and she had spent most of her time trying to make him happy.

As a teenager, she had had no interest in boys, and the few dates she had in college had come to nothing. Certainly none of the men that had come into her life had made her grip her cup and saucer as if she were going to crush them any minute like she was doing right then.

What's wrong with me? she asked herself, and wondered if the question should not have been *What's right with him?* The second question was the crux of her problem, she knew, and would take so much longer to answer.

His looks weren't the prime factor, she decided, though they were enough to start many women dreaming over him, as Iris had admitted to doing. Jamie had known several strikingly attractive men, yet had never been drawn to them. More than his looks, a magnetism seemed to emanate from him, drawing her as surely as the mythical sirens had been accused of drawing sailors to their deaths.

Tom put his cup down and half turned, crossing one well muscled leg over the other, giving her a lazy look. Behind those light eyes she seemed to see clouds of thought, too opaque for reading, but transparent enough to show that his mind was on more than his expression allowed to show. He raised his right arm, resting it on the back of the sofa, his elbow crooked. He lifted a strand of her long hair and fingered a curl.

'What did you sell in that discount store?' he asked softly.

'Oh, everything,' Jamie answered vaguely, wondering if she should draw away, knowing she wanted to stay where she was. With the strand of hair he touched her cheek, made a path of sensation along her jawline and down her neck. Her skin tingled. She felt a shiver of excitement go through her. Her fears were fighting for a foothold, but they were being shaken to the bottom of her mind.

'Clothes?'

I'm keeping them on! she thought in a panic, and realised he was still talking about the store.

'Sports clothes,' she said, hoping that would draw him off the subject. She would be in hot water again before she knew it if she tried to answer his questions, especially with that tendril of hair setting her skin aflame, and his eyes constantly boring into hers.

She tried avoiding his gaze, but turned towards him, he seemed to fill her area of vision. One arm lying negligently across his knee seemed to form a blockade on the other side of his broad shoulders. She felt as if she was surrounded by his masculinity, and if she raised her eyes to his again, she was going to be lost in her own emotion. Resolutely she jerked her eyes away and fixed her stare on the Ming bowl.

'What brands?' he murmured softly, and she was drawn back to the conversation that seemed to have pauses of minutes between the questions and replies. And who, talking business, used a voice that low, inviting, enticing? He was making her head reel.

'Oh, Fraziers, Lamworth, California Sun—' she named a few brands she knew.

'In a discount store?'

Too late she remembered they were exclusive shop brands. Her heart sank, knowing she had really made a mess of her answer. But by what right did he expect her to make sense when he was driving her crazy with that strand of hair?

'Sorry, brands I checked in today,' she fibbed. 'I guess I'm not in the mood to talk business.'

That was the *wrong* thing to say, she thought, but the words were out before she could stop them.

'I agree to that,' he replied instantly, and she raised her head to see his reaction. His half smile dissolved into an enigmatic expression as he leaned forward. His hand freed the strand of hair and slid behind her neck, pulling her towards him. His lips met hers, softly, experimentally, and with a fast growing urgency. His mouth explored hers, playing gently, building a sensitivity that made her tingle down to her toes.

But gathering behind that little thrill was a tidal wave of emotion, desire that flowed upward, threatening to envelop her completely. So sudden and fierce was the feeling that it frightened her, causing her to struggle against him and pull away.

She almost fell as she tried to slide away from him and get to her feet at the same time. Sure he could read every emotion in her face, she blushed a fiery red.

'Sorry I didn't have dessert,' she said, turning away,

'but around here, some things aren't on the menu.'

Tom slowly got to his feet. He seemed to be suppressing some emotion, but when he met her eyes, that lazy humour was back again.

'Sorry,' he said, and walked across the room to pick up his jacket.

Jamie stood irresolutely in the middle of the floor. Once she had broken away from his embrace, she knew she wanted to be back in his arms, but now it was too late. Her panic had destroyed the mood. Now what was she going to do?

He unhurriedly put on his coat and walked to the door.

'If the car gives you any more trouble, just shout. Possibly it wasn't the battery after all, but I think that was the problem.'

'Thank you for your help, I'm sure I'll be okay now.' Jamie's remarks were equally banal.

She followed him to the door, wondering what to say. She couldn't ask him if she would see him again. She didn't want to risk a negative answer. Out in the hall, he gave her that half smile she was beginning to know, and strolled towards the entrance of the building. She reluctantly closed the door.

So what am I protecting? she asked herself. But already she knew the answer. She was looking after Jamie Stone, because out of that door was walking a man who could crush that stone to gravel. Not because he would want to, or meant to, but she realised she had suddenly become frighteningly vulnerable. Around Tom Malcomb, all her strength and sense of self-preservation seemed to dissolve.

CHAPTER THREE

'How did you manage?—no—you didn't go out there and run the battery down on that car?' Abel Malcomb asked in a low voice.

George Stone looked around, making sure no one was close enough to hear their conversation. They were walking through Stone & Stone on the way to a restaurant that was known for its on-premises bakery and excellent breakfast rolls. At only minutes after nine o'clock, very few customers were on the floor, and there was particular silence about the store. Not even the call bells had started.

'No, that was a lucky break.' George led the way around the huge old mahogany cases in the men's department. 'And he had dinner with her?'

'Yea.' Abel slowed, lifted a shirt from a rack and examined it. 'George,' he said as he held the shirt in front of him, eyeing the result in a mirror on the other side of the counter, 'there's something wrong with this younger generation. When we were young, we could lie our way out of hell. Tom said last night they were falling all over each other—he flat out asked about her uncle, and she tangled her tongue more times than he could count. Good-looking shirt—wonder if we have one in my size?'

George looked at the label and shook his head. 'New brand, our new buyer came up with it. They get along okay?'

Abel shook his head. 'Tom doesn't tell me much, of course, but I'd say not. By his face I think something went wrong. Sure I don't have this shirt?'

'No, you don't—you couldn't get a hint from him?'

'Now, wouldn't he be a louse if he kissed and told?' asked Abel, walking over to a counter where a young clerk was trying to look interested. When Abel took out his wallet and handed over Malcomb's employee discount card, the boy looked puzzled for a moment, then indignant.

'Sir, we do not honour Malcomb's discounts here.'

George choked back a laugh as Abel glared at the clerk. Then shoving the card back in his wallet, he turned to George, his face red with anger. The cuffed sleeves waved in the air as he thrust shirt, hanger and all at George.

'I never buy without my discount! *You* pay for it!'

As the hands of the clock moved towards noon, Jamie looked down at the clipboard in her hand with some satisfaction. She had learned how to handle those irritating little perforated strips of paper, protect them from the occasional gusts of wind, dodge the truck drivers with their handcarts and boxes, and keep up the records. A few more good days to make up for her bad start, and she could tell Uncle George to shove his job.

But she wanted to leave with her head high. First she had to obliterate all memory of her first day. When she left, she wanted no doubt in anyone's mind that she could have handled the job with one hand if she chose to.

'Honey, are you ready to go?' Velma's head appeared in the window of the firewall where the belt entered the pricing section.

'Just let me wash my hands,' Jamie called back. She made her last entry and took the board back to the office where Freddy could find it if any shipments came in while she was at lunch. Lunch was another thing she could point to with pride when she told Uncle George that she really didn't need that six months on the tread-mill.

She joined Velma, Iris and Llewellyn every day, and there were certainly no three people with whom she could have less in common. She managed to hold her own with Llewellyn's blushes every time she looked at Rick, Iris's panting over nearly every man she saw, and Velma's constant chatter about her exploits. According to her she had been out with half the men in town who were worth dating, and three-quarters of those that weren't.

Jamie found the conversation a little limited and not what she could call stimulating, but it was at times enlightening. When she heard Iris's sighs and watched Llewellyn turning an unbecoming pink every time Rick came into the room, she was glad she had something else to occupy her mind.

Or something better was supposed to be occupying her mind. The business should be taking up her time and thoughts, but actually, she was no better off than they were. Tom Malcomb kept intruding in her thoughts with a regularity that was surprising and irritating, especially since he wasn't intruding into her life.

She was starting a new week, and she had only seen him to speak to once since he had left her apartment that night. The next day she had located him in his own warehouse, where she accosted him, wallet in hand, and demanded to pay for the battery. He had been with two of his people, so he had been casual, friendly, and gave no hint about whether he had left the apartment angry with her, or just amused. Jamie was half convinced it was the latter. But certainly he was not wasting any more time on her.

When she came out of the ladies' room after making some hasty adjustments to her appearance, she joined Velma and the two girls as they crossed the street between the trucks. Monday, it seemed, was always the busiest day, and on foot was the fastest way to travel in the warehouse district.

They were through the line and at a table when she saw Tom come in.

'There's that gorgeous hunk of money and masculinity,' Iris sighed.

Velma arched one pencilled brow. 'Iris, honey, you're crazy! Turn those words around. Not even money is as important as masculinity. Take it from one who knows.'

'Today I've got money on my mind,' retorted Iris. She stopped forking in the mashed potatoes and gravy long enough to reach in her pocket and pull out an advertisement, clipped from a magazine.

'For five thousand dollars I could go to that spa and come out like Twiggy in three months,' she said, handing the paper to Jamie.

'Honey,' said Velma in accents of extreme patience, 'If you want to look like Twiggy, stop travelling that line—' Velma pointed to the stainless steel counter, 'past the salad bar.'

'Pain and torture!' Iris made a face.

'Honey, if you consider that too much pain, I got news for you—those places have to be torture in posh. No one can make it fun to lose weight.'

'It might be worth it to get Tom Malcomb to notice me,' Iris sighed.

Llewellyn, who was usually quiet, looked up from her daily bowl of soup. 'You're getting as bad as Cleo about the diets.'

'Who?' asked Jamie, her interest only mildly piqued by the new name. Most of her interest in the conversation had evaporated with Tom's entrance into the cafeteria.

'Cleo Knowles,' Llewellyn answered. 'She had your job until she was transferred to the bulk warehouse.'

'Work is probably easier,' Jamie answered, just to be saying something.

'She didn't want to go,' Llewellyn said thoughtfully, as if she was wondering what had happened.

During this conversation, Jamie had kept her eyes on the brightly coloured ad Iris had handed her, but her mind was not on either the talk or the paper. She was directing her eyes so she could keep control of their action. Anything was better than letting her gaze stray towards Tom Malcomb, trying to locate where he was sitting, looking up at every bite to see if he was looking in her direction. She had been doing too much of that, and she was sure Velma had noticed. That woman, she thought, came equipped with romantic radar!

She couldn't resist one look around the room. He was sitting two tables away, his back to her. Well, no worry that he might not be able to keep his attention on his own table, she thought. As soon as she had finished her lunch, she excused herself and hurried back across the street.

Working with a will to forget her disappointment, Jamie logged in all the shipments, kept her records up to date, and even helped to load cartons on the belt, until Tom Malcomb came through the door that led to the back of the Stone & Stone building. He carried a long, flat carton in each hand. Both had been crushed and obviously pulled from the rubbish pile.

'Scrounging, Tom?' Hugh Belmont was at the other end of the platform, and he strolled over.

'I told you that shipment from Roselle had come in,' said Tom, putting the two crushed boxes down on the belt that was at the moment not in use.

Despite her discomfort at being close to Tom, Jamie couldn't resist taking a look at the boxes, especially since Tom had laid them down close to her.

Both boxes carried the logo of Roselle, a famous and

exclusive dressmaker, but one box was addressed to Stone & Stone, while the other had been sent to Malcomb's.

Hugh, a tall, cadaverous figure, with more hollows than flesh, scratched his sparse grey hair. 'Don't have any answers. Boxes in the trash?'

'Umm,' Tom nodded absently as he removed the crushed cardboard from the belt.

'I don't understand,' said Jamie, looking from the boxes to Tom.

'They were left off here along with your shipment. Obviously no one noticed a couple of extra boxes in the rush. Happens sometimes.'

Both men turned to the door that would take them into the adjoining area, where the dresses would have been unpacked, priced, and hung in an enclosed wardrobe cart. They would have been set upstairs for storage or taken directly to the stores by the company trucks that used the other end of the loading platform.

Jamie went back to work. She was surprised at her disappointment when Tom walked off with Hugh without giving her any personal attention.

What did you expect, a Valentine and roses? she asked herself, irritated that she was giving him so much attention. She busied herself stacking the boxes on the belt until Hugh and Tom appeared again, and Hugh shouted for her to accompany Tom up to the third floor.

She walked over, trying to hide her confusion behind her surprise.

'I'm not familiar with the third floor,' she said. Knowing she would be even more uncomfortable when alone with Tom, she was looking for an excuse not to go.

'He knows where he's going, you just trot along and help him look,' Hugh ordered, and turned away, expecting his directions to be carried out with no argument.

You just wait until you know who I am! Jamie thought.

Then she waved that idea aside. He was making what he thought was a perfectly reasonable request; how was he to know her feelings? She followed Tom as he led the way through the door from which he had first appeared.

The traffic on the receiving platform had kept Jamie too busy to do any exploring, so she was surprised when they came to the elevator shafts. One housed a large freight elevator, but the other shaft was open, and in its interior she could see a complicated system of hooks and cables.

'What's that?' she asked, forgetting her discomfort in her curiosity.

'That's part of the Wonder Child,' answered Tom. 'Haven't you seen it work?'

'No,' Jamie answered slowly. The word was hardly out of her mouth before a clatter came from around the corner and one of the numerous merchandise carts appeared, its wheels a foot off the floor as it rode the overhead monorail. The cart swung slightly as the rail curved to make a direct approach to the open shaft, and as it rode the rail inside the shaft, it was neatly snagged by the rising hooks attached to the cables.

As it disappeared up the shaft, Jamie took a step forward, but Tom's hand on her arm pulled her back.

'Careful, don't fall in,' he warned.

She stepped back hastily, feeling in the touch of his hand the memories of the night less than a week before. She fought to keep her attention away from him.

'Where is it going?' she asked, at the moment not really caring, but feeling the need to keep to a safe subject.

'I don't know, I didn't look,' he said, smiling down at her as if he knew what she was doing. That made her half angry. He could at least have the decency not to notice!

'Don't be funny,' she snapped.

'I'm not funning,' said Tom as he held the door of the

freight elevator for her. 'I could have told you if I'd noticed the dial at the top of the cart.' Those pale eyes were still amused, but he sounded serious.

Jamie remembered seeing the clock-like dials on the top of the carts, but she wasn't aware that they could be set for a destination. She had been so busy trying to keep up on the receiving platform, she had not had time to get curious over other things.

'You'll see what I mean when we get up on the third floor,' Tom told her, and Jamie had to be satisfied with that.

They rode the rest of the way in a forced silence, both protecting their personal space by half turning away from the other. When the door opened Jamie found it a relief to be on the huge, silent floor where she did not feel trapped with Tom.

She waited for him to lead the way, but he turned towards the open shaft and stopped at the railing that extended across the shaft.

'How do the carts get out?' she asked, and even as she spoke she saw her answer. The monorail was much higher off the floor as it left the elevator, and five feet out it dipped sharply, bringing it again down to a workable level.

She didn't know if the cart that appeared was the same one she had seen go into the elevator, but she watched with fascination as it came rolling off the lift, rode down the incline and started off across the expanse of concrete floor. Rails branched off to either side, and about half-way down the room the cart suddenly took a sweeping curve and parked itself near the wall along with several others.

'And you're telling me that thing knew where it was supposed to go?' Jamie demanded.

Tom laughed. 'You want to be sure? Come on – and stay out from between those painted strips.'

For the first time she saw the meaning of the parallel stripes on the floor. They delineated the path taken by the carts on the monorail. As Tom strode across them without slackening his pace, she couldn't resist a taunt.

'You didn't look both ways,' she said.

'I don't have to unless the fire alarm goes off,' he replied.

'Then what happens?' Jamie was glad as she asked her questions that he didn't know she was a Stone. She felt she should have known the answers, but the complicated programmed relay system had been installed just after her father's accident. She had been too young to know there was a warehouse, or even a company.

'They're just like people, stampeding to get out,' Tom replied. 'All previous programming is cancelled, and everybody makes for the door.'

'Wouldn't they get jammed up?' she asked.

'They're not that stupid. They go just like school kids, one class, or in our case, one department at a time, the most expensive ones first – those in the vaults on the second floor—if the fireproof door happens to be open.'

Jamie stayed quiet. She didn't even know there were vaults on the second floor. She decided she had a lot to learn about her business.

By that time they had caught up with the cart, and Tom unclipped the fastenings that held the canvas side closed. Inside were Narragansett sports shirts. Tom grinned as he pointed out the labels.

'Take a good look,' he said, refastening the clips. The next cart, when opened, showed the same brand. 'Probably going to one of the branches,' he said. 'Yeah, a repeat in sizes.'

'Then I take it back,' she murmured. 'They do know where they're going.'

'Uh-huh,' Tom's eyes were glinting again. 'And when *they* start out, *they* continue to their destination.'

That was a direct reference to the incident in her apartment, Jamie knew. Now how did she answer that?

'Like you said, they are *not* people,' she replied casually. 'They're programmed to respond, they have no choice.'

'Right, only people turn around in mid-stream,' he agreed.

'Always a good idea when the current is running a little swift,' Jamie retorted.

'Or when the wader can't swim?' Tom asked.

'Or doesn't choose to,' she said. 'I thought we came to look for dresses.'

'Well, it's certain we came to look for something,' he replied, taking a step towards her.

Jamie leapt back out of his way—and blushed furiously when instead of advancing on her, he walked right by, crossing the path of the main monorail before he paused. Keenly aware that she had made a tactical error, she followed behind, wondering just how many times she was going to be made to look foolish in his eyes. And it was all her own doing. Her eyes had been on the floor, making sure she stayed out of the area between the parallel stripes, and almost ran into him before she stopped.

Score another for dummy here, she thought as she stepped hastily aside. There must have been half an acre of concrete floor and she had to head for the exact spot where he stood.

'I thought you knew where you were going,' she groused.

'I do—in reverse,' he said thoughtfully, raising a finger to point. 'Three, five, six, seven—that branch,' he said, starting purposefully back towards the elevators. Again Jamie followed.

Tom explained as they walked. 'The systems are exactly the same, only in reverse because of the buildings. And before you ask, yes, Stone & Stone put theirs in first. This is one time Malcomb's picked the idea up from you people.'

'I wasn't going to say anything,' she objected. But Tom had reached the storage area he had been looking for, and the carts, on the round end of the branch, resembled a pioneer wagon train, circled and prepared against an attack.

'There are twenty carts here,' said Jamie. 'Do we search every one, looking at dress labels? This certainly isn't efficient.' She cringed as Tom gave her a sly look. She had said too much again.

'Normally we wouldn't have to. The receiving records for each shipment show the number of the cart—' Jamie had noticed the stencilled numbers on the equipment. 'But the papers are in transit to the buyer's office, so it's searching time. My buyer is livid—she's promised two of those dresses for this afternoon.'

'And Malcomb's always delivers,' said Jamie, thinking of the carts they would open, the hangers they would push aside in order to read each and every label.

'When a Malcomb gets a chance,' he said softly.

Jamie's eyes flew to his face, an action she immediately regretted. His eyes were slightly darker than usual, the slight curve to his lips enticing; not quite a smile—rather a wish, as if he was reliving a memory with both pleasantness and regret. Her feelings were betraying her again, she could feel that tingle building up. She fought against it by whirling around to the first cart and flipping the catches on the canvas side that served as protection of the clothing inside.

'Ro—Ro—' she cleared her throat to get rid of the lump that threatened to choke her. 'Roselles, you said?'

'Right.'

She started searching with a vengeance. The sooner they found those plaguey dresses and Tom was on his way, the better. She couldn't understand why he affected her so strongly, but he was too dangerous to have around when they were alone, she decided. And that was another thing. He could be so cool when he was down on the platform in front of everyone else, not giving anyone an inkling of his thoughts. Did he think she was someone he could see on the sly and pretend not to know in public? She wasn't having any of that! The thought made her so angry she pulled one of the dresses completely off the hanger and had to stop and rearrange the clear plastic dust cover that fitted over the shoulders of the dress like a cap.

That irritated her too, and in the next cart, she dislodged another dress, causing it to fall to the bottom of the cart. When it fell, the hanger came free of the garment, clattering against the metal frame inside the canvas sides. She was head and shoulders inside the dark interior, groping for the lost hanger, when she heard Tom shout. She didn't hear him clearly, and he had no time for a second warning.

Suddenly she heard a clang and was jolted off balance. Before she could right herself another clang reverberated from the metal frame and she was out of the cart, going over backwards. Just as she was about to fall, Tom caught her, moved a pace with her until he stopped her momentum, and in one fluid motion lowered both of them to sit on the concrete floor.

'You okay?' he asked, his arms still around her.

'I think so,' she answered, gingerly touching the side of her head, where the metal frame of the cart had grazed her. She could feel a slight soreness, but no lump. The ringing in her hears stopped almost immediately.

'One thing you learn with this system is not to be an ostrich when carts are incoming!'

Jamie turned her head towards the opening in the circle, and saw a new arrival heading down the branch to join those already there. It came to an abrupt stop as it hit the still carts. The others bumped together like railroad cars, and the reaction chained around the circle.

She shook her head, thinking she could have been slammed to the concrete if Tom had not caught her. She wanted to thank him, but somehow the words refused to come. His arms were still encircling her, but instead of protecting her from hurt, there seemed to be a subtle change in his hold, and the fingers of his left hand were gently moving as they touched her waist. Her sensitive skin, protected by the cotton blouse, was oblivious to the fact that his hands had met an obstruction. It tingled with all the reaction he could have desired.

With his right hand he lifted her chin and gently placed a quick kiss on her lips. Another and another followed before, caught up in his magnetism and her own desire, she was able to command herself to break free.

'I think we'd better get back to the job,' she said breathlessly.

'Let's make sure they've stopped sending carts first,' he murmured, planting kisses on her forehead.

'I think they've stopped, I don't hear any on the rail,' she countered, but even though she knew her answer to be correct, and logic said he was just stalling, she couldn't make herself force the cessation of those wonderful kisses.

But someone else could, she discovered. In the distance the sound of footsteps brought Tom's head up. Almost immediately he was on his feet, holding out his hands to help her.

'You're right, we had better get back to work,' he grinned. 'Don't want to be caught fraternising with the enemy! My people might not let me live it down.'

Without a word, Jamie turned back to the cart she had been searching and retrieved the hanger. She re-hung the dress and continued her search, doubly anxious not to waste a moment finding that shipment of dresses. The sooner she was away from Tom Malcomb the better. She decided he was three kinds of a louse and was playing a game with her. She wasn't someone he—or anyone else—could see on the sly, and he was going to learn that at the first opportunity!

There they were: the Roselle originals.

'I've found them!' she announced.

'Great,' he said, turning from the cart he was just ready to open. 'Good girl!' His arm fell around her shoulders, his eyes soft as he looked down at her.

Well, why not? she thought. *The footsteps have faded away, there's no one around.* She jerked away and frowned at him.

'There are the dresses, do as you like with them, but get one thing straight, buster, I don't have time for men who think they're too good to be seen with me!"

She stormed away, heading for the lighted stairway exit light that glowed at the end of the room. Had she made any sense? she wondered. What she said didn't quite seem to fit the facts. She really wouldn't care to have someone walk up when she was locked in an embrace with Tom, would she? Don't question, she warned herself. Right or not, it was necessary.

To add to her troubles, the stairway between the second and third floors did not continue to the street level. She could see the elevator shaft, but nothing was going to entice her to ride if she might have to share the car with Tom Malcomb.

'I'll stay lost in here until Uncle George sends a search party,' she fumed, 'but I will *not* put up with that man!'

Then a fallacy in logic occurred to her and the irritation became greater.

'And I don't have to,' she announced to the carts rolling by on the monorail. 'It's *my* warehouse!'

She was just considering the stupidity of that remark,

and the trouble it would cause if anyone had heard it, when an elderly man appeared from behind a partition. Knowing she had been heard, she slumped in defeat, but he just smiled and shook his head.

'Not quite right,' he chuckled. 'When they want it cleaned, it's all mine.'

The smile Jamie returned was full of relief, as she thanked her lucky stars she had been misunderstood.

He pointed out the stairway and she descended to the street level. She was somewhere near the back of the building, she guessed, seeing the ceiling-high bins that held banded stacks of bags and boxes. She took the first hallway she encountered and was on familiar territory when she spotted the door to the ladies' lounge.

As luck would have it, Velma was just coming out. She took one look at Jamie and reached behind her, opening the door again.

'I think, honey, you'd better come in here and we'll have a little talk.'

'Thanks, but I've got to get back to the platform.' Jamie tried to smile and knew it wasn't successful.

'That platform was taking care of itself years before you came along, sugar, and it will years after you leave. You come in here.'

Faced with Velma's insistence, Jamie capitulated and followed the older woman into the small room with its vinyl-upholstered furniture. When Jamie took a chair, Velma pulled one up closer, staring at her with shrewd eyes.

'It's Tom Malcomb, ain't it?'

'What?' Jamie was too surprised to answer, thinking her first analysis of Velma had been right. The woman really did have romantic radar!

'Dearie, let's face it. Here we're like a small town. Nothing goes on in either warehouse we don't know about. Everybody knows he helped you out with your car—'

'How—'

'Honey, you went over there and paid him for the battery, didn't you? I'll clue you in, it didn't take two hours for that to make the rounds. He's pretty cool, and I'll give you credit, you are too, but an old warhorse in the battle of love notices things.' Velma shifted, getting comfortable. 'I tell you, honey, the second he enters that door at the Grease and Glob, his eyes start making the rounds of the tables to see if you're there, just like my fifth husband.'

'Now, Velma—'

'And the way you watch for him,' the older woman went on obstinately, 'reminds me of me with my *first*.'

Jamie tried to speak again, but Velma waved away her objections.

'Now you've been upstairs with him, and you come down looking as if you've lost your last friend—I know you like him, honey, but believe me, that man is going to be poison in your life. You'd do better to forget him.'

Jamie had told herself the same thing on the third floor, and while she wanted to resent Velma's intrusion into what was certainly none of her business, she was grateful that the woman was so concerned about her.

'Thank you,' she replied, 'but I've come to that conclusion myself. If I never see that louse again, I couldn't care less. He's the most despicable man I've ever known!'

'Oh, damn!' Velma breathed, falling back against the vinyl upholstery and closing her eyes. 'I didn't know it had gone that far. I guess we'd better see what we can do about making it work for you.'

'I just said I never want to see him again,' Jamie protested.

'It ain't what you said, honey, it's the way you said it. That's exactly the way I felt about my first three husbands—and the sixth.'

CHAPTER FOUR

JAMIE spent the next two days trying to avoid any more private talks with Velma. She had a vision of the woman trying to persuade her to bleach her hair and make a run on a cosmetic counter. Butterflies and tiny satin bows might do for the supervisor of the pricing department, but the idea of wearing them herself sent her into shudders.

Velma's interest and concern with what she considered Jamie's route to happiness left Jamie with a warm feeling and a lot of confusion that had nothing to do with Tom. All during her school years, she had watched the girls around her dividing into couples and small groups of best friends and confidantes. Busy with her father, and proud of her professional, businesslike attitudes, she had been slightly contemptuous of those relationships. Strange, she thought, how she could be taught what she had missed by a brassy refugee from the nineteen-fifties.

Still, she was not going to let Velma turn her into someone entirely different from her nature. And certainly there was no point, she told herself. Not that she intended to change her image for any man, but if she did, it would not be for Tom Malcomb. She was determined to ignore him, to let him know he was the most forgettable man ever to enter her life.

The thought was good, but she found it hard to act upon an idea when apparently he had thought of it first. All day Tuesday and most of Wednesday, he was totally out of sight. Even when Hugh sent her over to Malcomb's warehouse to see if an overdue shipment had

70

been delivered to them by mistake, he was nowhere to be seen; nor did he come to the Grease and Glob for lunch.

Wednesday afternoon, when Jamie was alone on the platform, a truck from one of the larger freight lines backed up to the loading platform, and the driver, a bearded giant with arms the size of small trees, came around the back of the truck and started opening the doors.

Since the cut-off time for receiving was five o'clock, and no one was around to put the shipment on the belt, Jamie started out of the office cubicle to send him on his way. But she hesitated when she saw the emblem on the back of his jacket. From what she remembered, that emblem identified an infamous motorcycle club. If she made him angry, was she likely to be followed home by a squadron of roaring bikes? She had heard too many stories.

Still, Jamie was not one to be intimidated. She picked up her clipboard, her only handy weapon, and stalked out to the truck. The bearded giant turned and faced her. His face broke into a childlike, shamefaced smile.

'I'm late,' he stated the obvious. 'But I'd sure appreciate it if you could take this shipment—I'll sure get hell back at the terminal if you don't.'

Jamie, ready to fight off a squad of bikers if necessary to protect her rights, quailed at the idea of stiffly rejecting the driver's request and being the cause of getting him into trouble. After all, what did one shipment matter? She agreed to accept it.

With a growing feeling of dismay, she watched him unload carton after carton of merchandise. Too late she remembered the warehouse rule about not leaving anything on the platform overnight. Both Carl and Freddy had left for the day, and Hugh had been called to a meeting. She was the only one left to deliver it to the pricing department.

To add to her problems, she was facing a miscellany—a late order of Easter candy that would have to be priced and sent to the store the next morning, and several dress and suit boxes. By now she had learned that those long, four-inch boxes held clothing. The varying sizes of square cartons could be anything, she thought as she logged in the candy, but with her luck, every size would be for a different department. And she had finished and totalled her reports, too.

'Thanks, ma'am,' the bearded giant said as she signed the shipping invoice and gave him back his copy. 'Sorry I was so late. You sure kept me out of trouble.'

You're out of trouble, but mine's just beginning, she thought as the truck pulled away, leaving her to stare down at the stack of boxes.

The easiest part of the job was changing her records, so while she gathered her strength for loading the belt, she made the additions to her closely written sheets and then totalled them.

'Well, nothing to it but to do it,' she quoted the words of the old song as she slid her paperwork into a manila envelope and dropped it in the inter-company mail slot at the end of the platform.

She had watched Carl and Freddy load the belt, and that just took muscle. No brains required. Three boxes for department fourteen were placed one after another, and a small space between so the next order didn't get on the conveyor until she was ready for it. Five boxes for department twenty-six—humm, department thirty-one, high fashion. She knew where those items would end up: on the same wagon train circle she and Tom had searched on Monday.

Don't think about Monday, she told herself.

When the belt was full she went over and flipped the

switch to turn on the system and stared at the myriad buttons that controlled the complicated mechanism. Something was missing. Where were the department numbers?

They had to have department numbers! How else was she going to send the shipments to the right pricing station?

Could she just run the stuff around the corner to get it off the platform and leave it on the belt? No! That would create trouble for Carl and Freddy in the morning.

Like an answer to her prayer, she heard footsteps on the concrete—nice, authoritative steps, taken by someone who was capable of making a decision. Maybe whoever it was would know how to run the conveyor. She turned around to see Tom Malcomb striding along with a bottle and two glasses in his hand, angling for Hugh Belmont's office. When he saw her he checked his stride, his expression momentarily hesitant, then he smiled.

'You still here?'

'No,' said Jamie, unable to resist the only possible answer to such a banal remark.

'Is Hugh still here—in the same sense?' he asked, his eyes lighting up.

'Yes,' Jamie answered, meaning, of course, that he was not, and Tom understood. He sighed as he looked down at the bottle and glasses in his hand. 'Then how would you like a day-capper?'

'Not my drink,' she said, 'and I can't cap my day until I get this stuff off the platform.'

'You took in a late shipment,' Tom accused.

'How did you guess?' Jamie was sarcastic. Her heart was doing funny little jigs, which were not in the rules for her new attitude to Tom Malcomb, and she was a little disappointed that those footsteps had not brought her a solution to her problem. Heart or no heart, at the moment she wanted help in getting that shipment off the platform.

'Tell you what,' said Tom, putting the bottle and the glasses down by one of the building support columns. 'You run the belt, and I'll load for you.'

'I don't know how to run it.' Jamie felt and sounded like a petulant child, and hated it. 'I've been busy learning other things,' she defended her ignorance.

'Shouldn't be too hard to figure out,' Tom muttered. 'I know I've seen a diagram of the pricing department. Hugh had one in his office—'

'I have that on my board,' she said, and ran for her small cubicle where her clipboard had been stored for the night. She came back flipping pages until she found the mimeographed sheet. Each pricing station was responsible for several departments, the numbers neatly listed in typed numerals.

'That should do it,' Tom nodded, looking over her shoulder. 'Just start here,' he pointed to the row of buttons. 'The stations and the buttons correspond, just work right along your diagram.'

That's not too bad, it's all in knowing how, Jamie decided. With a confident finger she pressed the control button for the receiving platform belt and brought her first boxes up to the control panel. A careful check to make sure she had counted off the pricing stations correctly, and she sent the first three cartons on their way. The next boxes were for department fifty-six. She checked her list and pressed her buttons, watching proudly as they rounded the corner.

By now she had cleared space on the end of the belt. Tom took off his coat and started loading the far end. In between the button pushing that sent the cargo to its destination, Jamie watched him as he worked. His smooth movements hid a tremendous strength, she thought. He made the heavy cartons appear to be—what had he called the pillows—boxes of feathers. She could see his light knitted shirt give as when he hefted a considerable weight, his muscular arms expanded slightly.

A little tremor went through her as she watched him. She thought of those arms that had held her only two days before, and how wonderful they felt.

That's not according to the new rules, she warned herself. Deliberately she turned her eyes away from him and back to the clipboard. She double-checked her diagram of the pricing stations. It wouldn't do to have the shipments end up in the wrong departments; the story would get back to Uncle George and she'd never hear the end of it. All she wanted was a few more days without incident and she was going to tell him to take his job—the rest he could figure out for himself.

When the last carton of Easter candy had been loaded, Tom walked over to where Jamie was confidently working the controls.

'Not too bad, is it?' he asked. She tried to ignore the sensation caused by his breath on the top of her head; this was no time to get nervous and make an error. She strove for a light tone to keep him from knowing how his closeness affected her.

'Not with someone to load,' she said gaily. 'This is one fabulous way to handle freight. Shame we can't run a belt out to the trucks, and save having to lift anything.'

'That's an idea, only we tried it and we didn't get it to work,' he admitted. 'Maybe we need you working on it.'

'I'll give it some thought,' she said as the last of the candy went through. 'How long will it take the last of these to get to their destination?'

'Just a minute or two. I'll watch.' Tom strolled around the end of the belt and stood at the low window where the belt entered the other area. Jamie, waiting for him to give her the word to shut the system down, watched his face change from a casual, pleasant expression to one of puzzlement, and on to trouble.

She felt a cold chill the evening didn't bring about.

'What is it?'

Tom shook his head. 'I don't think the chocolate Easter bunnies belong in the fashion section.'

'What?' Jamie felt her adrenalin surge.

'I think we goofed.'

'But I followed the diagram exactly,' she insisted, using one finger to stab at the sheet on the clipboard.

Tom turned from the window and laid his coat over the handle of a handcart. He started rolling up his sleeves.

'Remember—' he spoke as if he dreaded the reaction his words would bring about, 'when I told you my system was in reverse?'

'You didn't take that into account?' Jamie stared at him, unbelieving.

'I didn't think about it.'

'I don't believe it!' she stormed. 'After this goof, I'll be stuck in this warehouse for—' she bit her tongue, holding back what she was going to say, but the spectre of Uncle George laughing at her brought fire to her eyes, and Tom Malcomb was responsible for it.

His eyes flickered, but apparently he had taken her to mean she would be delayed while she corrected the error in the pricing department.

'There's nothing for it but to get in there and straighten it out,' he said. 'But I won't leave you to do it by yourself.'

'Thanks,' said Jamie, and walked around the belt and stepped over the low sill. She knew she could have sounded more grateful. She was grateful—after all, he meant well. Anyone could forget. 'Sorry, I meant that to sound genuine. It was meant that way.'

'Are you folks through here?'

Jamie turned to see the security guard by a switch box on the outside walls.

'Yea, close them up,' called Tom, and Jamie watched as the large bay doors lowered with a rumble and terminated in a slam that echoed through the building.

'They should have been closed before,' she grumbled. 'Then we wouldn't be in this mess.'

'We?' Tom faked a big surprise. 'I'm not in any mess.'

'Now wait a minute,' she looked up, not sure whether or not he was joking. He looked perfectly serious. 'Who told me how to work the belt—with what result?'

'Didn't they tell you when they hired you not to listen to the competition? Following my directions doesn't alleviate your blame, it compounds it.'

'Well, I'm readjusting my opinion of you,' she retorted. 'I thought all along you were a spy. Now I see you're a saboteur as well!'

She had ducked under the framework of the belt and stood in the middle of the pricing section, looking around. Of the sixteen planned stations, only eight were being used. She supposed the rest were put in operation during the Christmas holidays. The clutter of empty boxes, crumpled tissue paper and packing insulation had been removed, but since the receiving platform had been busy during the afternoon, most of the eight tables had boxes waiting for the morning. Across the foot of the off ramps, where they connected with the long, metal-topped tables used for opening and unpacking shipments, bars kept the incoming cargo from crowding the table. All the bars were up with the exception of the one in the section where a number of long flat dress and suit boxes were stacked, and several larger, flimsier cartons. The heavy boxes of candy had been sent down that ramp. With no bar to stop their speed, they had tumbled off the smooth surface of the table.

'No, it couldn't happen,' Jamie muttered, starting in

that direction. A candy box had fallen off, its corner crushing one of several hat boxes that had been removed from the packing carton but had not yet been put on a carrier. She knelt and lifted the lid. Underneath was a straw hat in glossy blue, crushed on top and boasting a broken white feather.

'I'm ruined,' she wailed. 'Just ruined!'

'Maybe we could tape it together—think anyone would notice?' asked Tom, looking over her shoulder.

'Don't be funny!' she snapped, getting to her feet. 'You don't know what that broken feather means to me. I thought if I did well on this job for a couple of weeks I could—I could—' She could walk out of the warehouse with her head high, face Uncle George down, and insist on her place on the board; but how could she when she had made a shambles out of trying to work on the receiving platform? And she couldn't explain it to Tom Malcomb, either. Her agreement with her uncle included getting along in the store with no one knowing who she was. Undoubtedly that meant Malcomb's too.

'Just take my word for it, I'm ruined!' She frowned up at him, caught between laughter and frustration. As upset as she was, her sense of humour would not let her get by with sounding like a heroine out of a nineteen-twenties movie. She tried to pass it off as a joke, and wrinkled her nose at Tom. 'You—you saboteur!'

She was expecting him to laugh too, but his eyes were surprisingly sympathetic. Instead of making a comeback to her barb, he stood staring off into the distance, ignoring her for a moment. Then he bent over the box again.

'Maybe things aren't as bad as you think. Let's get this junk shifted around, put on the right ramps, and then I've got an idea.'

'An idea? There's no way you're going to mend that feather.'

'Just move boxes,' he ordered. 'Heaviest Easter bunnies I've ever seen!'

'They're not bunnies,' said Jamie after bending over to read the shipping label. 'They're boxes of assorted chocolates. That accounts for the weight.'

Ten minutes later they had sorted out the shipments, and re-checked to make sure all the cartons were on the proper ramps. Jamie stood back, wondering if they had left any evidence of their fiasco. But of course they had. The hat box was dented, the hat ruined, and the pricing clerk could not be left to take the blame.

She would have to confess to Hugh in the morning, and by afternoon, she was sure her uncle would know all about it. He seemed to know everything, and she had yet to figure out where he got his information.

Tom came to stand by her as she stared at the hat.

'Do you have a coat?'

'Of course not, it's too warm for a coat,' Jamie said.

'See if you can find one. If not a coat, a jacket.'

'Why?'

He grinned down at her. 'Do you want to hide your awful secret, or don't you?'

'I have a jacket, but—'

'Then don't ask questions, just go get it.'

As she hurried away she took her clipboard, the last bit of evidence, other than the hat, that she had been in the vicinity. When she came back she was shrugging on the light garment.

'Take it off!' Tom insisted. She noticed he had the crushed hat in his hand. 'Here, take this—now, fold the jacket over your hand like this—'

Jamie stood still for him to arrange the garment so that the hat was hidden. But she objected to the obvious.

'It's not enough we ruined it, now we're going to steal it?'

Tom bared his teeth in a pseudo-grin. 'Now we're

going to trade it—at least, I hope we're going to trade it. We have the same supplier, you know. Maybe we have the same model.'

'If we could—' Jamie's hope died. 'No. If I don't 'fess up over here, then *our* price clerk gets in trouble. If the hat's over in Malcomb's section, *yours* does. I won't do it. If we could go somewhere and buy one, it would be different, but I won't let someone else take the blame.'

'I'll pick up the flak. I'm not brand new on the job, I don't *think* they'll fire me over one hat.' He put his arm around her shoulder, giving her a strictly supportive and brotherly hug. 'And it's my fault anyway. I gave you the wrong directions on the belt.'

'That's right, and you need to pay for your evil deeds,' Jamie said, smiling up at him. 'Let's go a'trading.'

She wasn't long finding out that the trading was going to be harder than it looked. Neither Stone & Stone nor Malcomb's was lacking in security guards. They left the pricing section without encountering anyone, but from there on they crept a few feet, stopped, and peered around corners to make sure the way was clear.

On the S. & S. platform they ran into their first check. They hid behind the wall of Jamie's office as they heard someone approaching. While they waited for the guard to pass, Tom slipped an arm around her shoulders again and bent his head to give her a kiss on the forehead.

'Hey, we're on a mission—as a spy, you should know to keep your mind on the objective,' murmured Jamie.

'I am,' he whispered back, giving her another kiss.

'We're supposed to be stealing a hat,' she argued, finding she too needed to remember their goal. The warmth of his body next to hers, his wide chest just a breath away, was sending her emotions whirling.

When the echoes of the footsteps had disappeared, they slipped through the door on the platform that led between the two warehouses, which for some reason inexplicable to Jamie was never locked.

In Malcomb's warehouse they waited in the corner while the guard travelled his route across the platforms before Tom could get into his office for a flashlight. Tom spent his time keeping Jamie jumping by feinting passes. She kept ducking away, fearing the security guard might turn at any time and see them. Her frowns and silent demands that Tom keep his mind on the business at hand only made his eyes gleam with mischief.

By the time he returned with the flashlight, she had begun to wonder if he was pulling some elaborate joke.

'Are you sure all this is necessary?' she asked, 'or are you just getting in a little sneaking practice?'

'For someone who's getting a free course in sneaking, you're not very appreciative,' he retorted. 'Now pipe down and pay attention to where we're going.'

He grabbed her hand and pulled her after him as he led the way up the dimly lit stair. On the third floor landing they opened the door a crack and listened.

'No footsteps, let's go,' he said.

Still holding her hand, he led her out into the darkness of the warehouse. Dimly, in the light from the windows, she could see the outlines of the carriers on the monorail. Only two lights were burning: the red light over the stairway, and one over the elevator. They left most of the stairway in darkness.

'Oh, I can just see it,' she muttered as she trudged along in the darkness. 'We'll be caught and the headlines will be two inches tall—because of who you are, of course.' And not only because of Tom's name, she added to herself. She didn't know, but they might put people in jail for using aliases. The headline would be: HEIRS TO MALCOMB'S AND STONE & STONE CAUGHT ROBBING WAREHOUSE.

'Spread it around, why don't you?' Tom whispered back, and his words only partially covered the echoes that were coming from all around her.

'Shh!' she admonished him, but she knew it would be too late if the guard had been on the third floor. The thought scared her and she reached for his hand.

He paused and one arm slid around her shoulders. The comfort it should have given her was negated by her alarm.

'What is it?' she whispered, just loud enough for him to hear.

'All this sneaking is tiring; let's take a break.' He kissed her again.

With the heel of her hand she pushed against his chest. 'Get on with it, before I go into screaming hysteria!'

'And I thought you were a brave little girl,' he murmured in her ear. Taking her arm, he continued along the floor.

Jamie walked closer to him than was strictly necessary. She needed to know he was there, she needed to feel his thigh as it brushed hers, to hear his effortless breathing. From the solidity of his presence she was drawing her courage.

Even in the dark, Tom was at home in his own warehouse. Before long they had stopped at a circle of carriers and he was busy checking the contents with the light. The search only took moments because only four carts were in the circle.

'Damn,' he said softly.

'It's not there,' said Jamie, doom in her voice. While he had searched, she had been watching the elevator and the stair well, thinking she made an efficient lookout. The time had passed with agonising slowness, but he had not been searching long enough to have found the hats and checked the boxes.

'The shipment's gone over to the main store,' he said,

his disgust clear in his growl. 'Maybe it's on the floor now.'

'They wouldn't *sell* it!' Jamie gasped, thinking how close they had come to replacing the mangled hat to hide the evidence of her error.

'Of course not! According to Dad and the board of directors, we don't sell anything,' Tom whispered back. 'Come on, I have some keys to the side door. We'll be back before you know it.'

She followed him as he led the way down a narrow flight of stairs. They were definitely not designed to the new building codes, so they must have been installed in the days when the old structure was built. Twice she nearly tripped, but his strong arm circled her waist. She was glad to let him play the strong role, leading her down in the darkness.

When they were outside in the alley and he had locked the door behind them, he looked down at her, his smile only half humorous. 'Last chance for a kiss.'

'Will you be serious? We're two inches from a trip up the river, and you want to be romantic!'

'What do you think I meant about last chance?' Tom complained.

His arm stayed around her as they walked along the dark alley until they came out on the street across from the parking lot. She was glad to lean back in the leather bucket seat of the Jaguar while he drove to the store.

A few minutes later they were hurrying across the second floor of Malcomb's, looking out of place among the thin mannequins in their high fashion outfits and the portly matrons and sales clerks who looked for larger sizes. Jamie caught sight of herself in a mirror and thought she definitely looked as if she had come out of a warehouse. She would have liked to comb her hair and tuck her shirt in neatly, but their mission was too desperate. Too many people were shopping for Easter hats.

'May I help you?' a clerk with blue-white hair, pink fingernails and the customary dark dress of the better departments accosted them as they inspected the trees of hats. Obviously she had looked them over and decided they should have been shopping in the basement where the markdowns were displayed.

'I'm looking for something in blue straw,' Jamie said confidently. For the fourth time since she had begun to breathe the rarified air of the *better* clothing department she reminded herself that she was, after all, Jamie Stone.

The saleswoman seemed suddenly pleased. 'Sorry, I don't believe we have a *thing* in blue straw.'

'Are you sure you don't have something?' asked Tom. 'Maybe some new merchandise not yet on the floor?'

He received a superior smile. 'Everything we have is out, sir. I'm very sorry. Have you tried the basement?'

One look at Tom's face and Jamie's mental headline changed: HEIR TO MALCOMB'S ATTACKS EMPLOYEE. S. & S. HEIR HOLDS COAT.

'Thank you, we will,' she said, grabbing Tom's arm and pulling him away. She didn't blame him for his anger, but they could not afford a scene.

He glowered as they walked off. 'Have you tried the basement?' he mimicked. 'She may be working there next week!'

'Maybe that shipment went to the branches,' Jamie moaned.

'Not on your life,' growled Tom. 'We haven't sent anything out to the branches for two days. If they left the warehouse, they came here. Now she's made me mad! I'm gonna have that hat!'

Jamie looked up at the firm jaw, the light grey eyes that had deepened, turning steely. His determination left her in no doubt that if there was a duplicate model, they were going to get it. She just hoped there was.

'What do we do now?' She was allowing herself to rely on him, she thought, and that was exactly what she had decided not to do. But it was pleasant, and she justified her lapse in independence by reminding herself it was his store, or more accurately, it would be one day.

'Look,' he said, pulling her to the side to look at a pair of high fashion shoes that would have maimed anyone who wore them. 'See that open door?'

Jamie looked back towards where a clerk was holding a door while a porter brought in a rack of dresses. In the service area, several carriers from the warehouse stood waiting to be unloaded.

'We can't get back there until the store is closed. Let's get something to eat before I bite an employee!'

'If that's what you do when you're hungry, I'm glad I don't work for you,' teased Jamie, her mind relived for the moment, knowing the hat wasn't going to be sold that night.

'Oh, I'll keep you for dessert.' He gave her a wolfish smile.

The scandalised expression on a passing customer's face warned Jamie he had been overheard. She choked back a laugh.

'We'd better get out of here before we demoralise the whole floor,' she muttered. 'But where can we go dressed like this?'

'There's a place I know not too far from here. They know me, so they won't mind.'

'The magic name of Malcomb's?' Jamie teased.

'It's good for something, at least it will get us in the door,' Tom said confidently as he led her to the escalator and across the busy main floor of the store. Jamie refrained from commenting on that bit of snobbery—after all, hadn't she recently recognised some in herself? She was glad she had reserved her comments because, after a five-minute walk up one of the major streets, they turned into a brightly lit area where a low building stood beneath enormous golden arches.

'You're a fraud!' she laughed as they walked up to the counter.

'*I* am?'

The clerk behind the counter chose that moment to ask for their order, so Jamie was left wondering what had brought on Tom's startled and disconcerted look. There was no opportunity to ask any questions as he ordered for both of them, after consulting her on her desire for cheese on her burger.

'Go find us a table,' he said, leaning against the counter as he waited for the order. 'And don't forget to tip the head waiter.'

Jamie had always been active, but the work on the platform was a little different from her accustomed activities, and by the end of each day she was tired and sore. She chose a booth by a window, and took her seat, glad to rest for a few minutes while Tom stood at the counter. His casual attention seemed to be on a brightly painted car in the parking lot, and a group of teenagers that were gathered around it. He leaned against the edge of the counter, relaxed, seemingly in charge of the situation, and she was willing to leave it that way.

He was a hunk, she thought, falling back on the term her generation had been using when she was in school. No wonder Iris sighed over him in her dreams! Jamie was willing to bet many of those dreams occurred when the stout girl's eyes were wide open.

As if you've just come to that conclusion, she chided herself.

In a few minutes he came to the table with a tray so loaded she understood the frown of the counter girl.

'Who's supposed to eat all that?' she asked, eyeing the boxes and cartons he put on the table.

'You'd be surprised. A spy eats when he can. You

never know when you'll get your next meal.'

'This one does,' said Jamie, choosing one of the larger boxes and opening it carefully. 'I'll fill my knapsack and have enough for a month.'

'And you'll be the second spy in history to be caught by a trail of ants.'

'Who's the first?'

'Guess,' he grinned, handing her a coke.

They entered the store at five minutes before nine and hurried to the bank of elevators. The starter took one look at Tom and led the way to the last car, the only one that led to the executive offices on the top floor.

'Shall I tell the guard you're in the building, Mr Malcomb?'

'Yes, I guess you'd better. Tell him I'll be in my office for a bit. Don't bother to come up, I can run the elevator.'

Once the door had closed and the car was rising Jamie turned to Tom.

'You have an office in the store?'

'Oh, sure. They don't let me hang my hat in it very often, but I have one.'

'But couldn't you insist? After all, you're—well, you're Tom Malcomb.'

'I'd be pretty stupid. I'll be stuck up there soon enough. Once you're up there the load just keeps on going and there's no time to get out. I don't mind waiting.'

As the doors slid open to show a long, empty corridor, Jamie waited for Tom to lead the way. Was he saying something she should think about? she wondered. She had been raised to accept that responsibility of the top floor, but then so had he. She knew he had travelled around the country, working in various jobs, not trying to build a career, but widening his experience before he had returned to Malcomb's a year before.

Since then he had held various positions in the business, and from what she had heard, not one of them had been in the administrative offices. She fleetingly wondered if he was deliberately shirking the responsibility, but the thought didn't fit the pattern. She watched him as he led the way down the silent, empty corridor. There was authority in his walk; his broad shoulders moved with the even rhythm of someone who had learned to carry responsibility.

She knew he was respected by the employees in the Malcomb's warehouse. They would have been the first people to turn on him if he had not been an able supervisor.

Tom Malcomb, she thought, was a very special type of man.

CHAPTER FIVE

JAMIE was still following Tom when they passed the bulwark of a desk in the middle of the passage. During the day it would be manned by some determined secretary or receptionist who guarded the occupants of the offices beyond. Jamie smiled, wondering what the well manicured, chic employee would think if she could see the disreputable couple sneaking past her desk.

Tom stopped at a door that bore his name. No title had yet been added, and she wondered if there would be one. Somehow he didn't seem the type to allow one on the door.

As he flipped the switch and the room was illuminated, she felt as if she was seeing another facet of his personality. Her first impression was one of solidity. The office seemed so completely one with itself, yet not a place to be noticed. She was looking at a monochromatic symphony where everything from the large walnut desk and console, carpeting and curtains, to the leather-upholstered chairs and couch, were in the same warm browns. The furnishings ranged from dark vibrant shades to pastels. Even the paintings on the walls carried out the colour scheme.

A casual glance would have told her she was looking at modern art of the finest quality, but the hangings were obviously chosen to blend, to add the finishing touch to the room without causing distraction. Here and there, satin finished brass and living plants added a warmth without intruding. She was standing in a room of power. From here, Tom would one day run the company he was born to head. Somehow, Jamie knew he would allow nothing to deter his purpose, just as the room allowed nothing to break his concentration.

No, she decided, looking around the room. *He won't evade his responsibilities when the time comes, and he'll never stint on his job or allow half measures.* Suddenly she was a little sorry for that nasty clerk on the second floor. She wouldn't escape his watchful eye, nor would or any other minor infraction of the dependability and attitudes that should personify Malcomb's. He was going to be her competition, and suddenly she was a little afraid.

'Have a seat,' he said, looking at his watch as he closed the door. 'By quarter past, the floors should be almost clear.'

But looking over the room, reading the connotations of what she saw, Jamie knew she was not going to be comfortable. This was a different Tom Malcomb from the man who had sneaked through the warehouse and eaten hamburgers in a moulded plastic booth. She walked over to a small table that held a thriving split-leaf philodendron and stood looking down at the plant.

She didn't hear him cross the room, but suddenly his hands were on her shoulders.

'Don't worry,' he said softly. 'We'll get a hat.'

'I'm not worried,' said Jamie, not wanting to turn, wanting to turn, needing to run, yet desiring more than anything to face him and hold him in her arms.

'Then relax. We'll be on our way in fifteen minutes,' he murmured into her hair as his hands moved slowly down her arms, caressing as they went. He was standing close to her, she could feel the warmth of him on her back and legs. She felt his breath as his head lowered, and a shiver went through her as his lips touched the back of her left ear.

Unnoticed by her, her knuckles were turning white as

she held on to the small table top with both hands. Waves of desire threatened to overwhelm her, frightening her with their intensity.

When his lips touched her neck, she could stand it no longer. Either she must turn towards him or get away.

'Keep your mind on getting that hat,' she said, trying to make her voice light—hard work, because it wanted to tremble. She ducked away, sidestepped, and was out of his hold in a moment.

'One thing spies should remember,' she said, hurriedly crossing the room. 'They should keep their minds on the problem at hand.'

'I am,' answered Tom as he strode after her.

Do something, Jamie warned herself, feeling desperate. 'What's your view like—you have to have a view?'

'Don't—' Tom warned, but he spoke too late. Her fingers closed on the traverse cord, flinging the curtain wide. Her view was of a lighted window directly across the street, where she saw her Uncle George handing a drink to a large man with leonine white hair. As he turned and would have faced the window, Jamie took the fastest opportunity to get out of sight. She dropped to the floor, for one panicky moment not caring what Tom Malcomb thought as long as her uncle didn't see her.

Oh, that was stupid, she told herself. Now he'd try to pick her up or something dumb, and Uncle George would watch her being hauled up off the floor.

But, surprisingly, Tom's first action was to close the curtains as far as she had opened them. When he came over to help her to her feet his eyes were amused, and there were no questions about why she had fallen. Obviously he had his own ideas.

'Sorry, I didn't know your office was monitored,' she said. No point in pretending she hadn't dropped out of sight deliberately. 'I wasn't sure what the reaction across the way might be—we don't need any curiosity about our mission,' she added, trying to blame the entire incident on the hat.

'No, that's the last thing we need,' Tom agreed. He was too quick with his answer, and the relief he felt was too obvious.

His attitude was strange sometimes, she decided, but since he wasn't asking any embarrassing questions, she certainly wasn't going to lead the conversation around to where he started having second thoughts.

'What's the time?' she asked.

He looked down at his watch. 'Ten past. We can start down the back way in a couple of minutes.'

'We don't want to cut it too close,' Jamie warned, thinking they were too near their objective to risk hurrying and getting caught.

'We won't,' Tom's face turned slightly hard, his eyes darkened, not to a steely grey, but a lighter shade, like some shining impervious alloy. 'That broad on the second floor is going to be in for a surprise!' As if he realised he was showing too much determination, he shrugged and added casually, 'And we'd better get back into the warehouses before too long. Be hell to go through all this and then have the security guards start asking questions.'

Jamie agreed and picked up the jacket, which still concealed the hat. Tom led her halfway across the building, past large rooms where every desk was either holding a computer or was in itself some giant piece of mechanised office equipment. Then he led the way down the stairs.

Twice they stopped on landings as they heard voices, and waited until the clerks and porters had drifted away in twos and threes. Most of the talk they overheard was about tired feet and whether to go straight home or stop for something to eat first.

When they reached the second floor, Tom led the way down the back corridor that was clogged almost to impassability. Racks of dresses, coats, evening wear and negligees lined the walls. Mingled among them were the warehouse carriers, some still holding new merchandise, some waiting to be taken back on the next truck. The obstructions they encountered most often were the low canvas-sided hampers that were used to haul everything from stock to laundry and equipment.

The hampers, approximately four feet long and about three feet wide, were the catch-alls for anyone who wanted to move anything. Their sturdy wooden platforms were supported by four heavy-duty wheels, set not at the corners, but at the centres of each side. Smaller wheels on the front and back made them easier to turn in tight places. The heavy metal frames, lined with sail canvas, could support considerable weight and bulk, making them useful for almost any load. Several were filled with purchases made that day by customers who preferred to have their new acquisitions delivered.

As they threaded their way through the clutter that serviced the neat counters and racks out on the sales floor, Tom stopped occasionally to peer through the small panels in the heavy service doors.

'The next one has to be the hat department,' he muttered as he continued along.

Jamie hoped he was right, since not far on the other side of the upcoming doors, the hall came to a dead end. She waited anxiously as he looked again, and sighed as he nodded. He eased the door open and she heard a familiar voice.

'I'll finish putting these out; you get the rest off the carrier.'

They made a mad scramble to get behind one of the low hampers and had just dropped to the floor when a clerk came through the double doors, propping one open as she left the sales floor. Peeping over the top of her cover, Jamie watched as she took a stack of hat boxes from the warehouse cart and returned, closing the door after her.

'*Now* they put them out,' muttered Tom through gritted teeth.

'At least it will be easier to find if it's on display,' Jamie said hopefully.

'Uh-huh, we'll get it, get out, and maybe the evening won't be a waste after all.' His arm slid over her shoulders.

'Keep your mind on that hat,' she said, crawling away to sit behind another cart. This one had been filled with some sort of sheeting. By the smell of dust in it, she guessed it had been used as a dust sheet for something just taken out of storage. She hoped she wouldn't be behind it too long, or the tickle of dust in her nose was going to explode in a sneeze.

'Coward!' Tom whispered.

Not trusting herself with a comeback, lest that sneeze get past her, she nodded vigorously.

But moments later he left his hiding place and went to the door. As he opened it a crack, she could hear receding voices. In a moment she was by his side, and less than a minute later they were on the sales floor, checking the hats.

While Jamie checked one side of the department, Tom looked over the other. In a moment she heard him speak.

'Is this it?'

She went over and stood shaking her head. 'It's almost the same, but it has two feathers, and the other had one, see?' She pulled out the damaged hat.

'Can't you break one off?'

Jamie frowned at him. Sometimes, men were definitely lacking in good sense!

'It looks close enough to me. Do they make them all the same?'

'Of course not!' She looked up at him, her mouth falling open in dismay. 'These are all originals! There's not going to be *another* one.' She collapsed on one of the ornate stools. Her strength and spirit drained away. She was no longer worried about being caught in the wrong by Uncle George. Both she and Tom had been through a lot that evening as they had tried to get another hat, and she felt the failure for both of them.

Tom looked as downcast as she felt. Then his eyebrows went up, and he snapped his fingers.

'If they're all different, who knows what the first one looked like? The hat hadn't been priced, so I bet it hadn't been opened. Who cares if it has one feather or two?'

Then again, sometimes men had very good sense—particularly Tom Malcomb.

'Nobody,' said Jamie with decision, and shoved the damaged hat on the blank-faced model head.

The hat was tucked under her jacket, and they had just entered the corridor again when they heard footsteps. Tom grabbed Jamie's hand and they went back into hiding behind the low canvas carriers.

'Another long night,' an abnormally deep voice said.

'Security guards,' Tom whispered in her ear.

'And do my feet hurt!' the other answered. 'You check in there, I'll take a look on the floor, and then we'll have some coffee in the corner.'

'What corner?' Jamie whispered to Tom. He looked around, made a wry face, and pointed to the table behind them. Two chairs were beside it, and sitting on top were two metal lunch boxes and two thermoses.

Headlines: HEIRS TO MALCOMB'S AND S. & S. CAUGHT STEALING HAT.

One set of footsteps seemed to be echoing in another

room and with the swing of the double doors, the other disappeared. Then Tom was on his feet, jerking Jamie up after him. Before she knew what he was doing he lifted her and unceremoniously dumped her in a canvas hamper. He stepped in with her, sat down, pulling her with him, while with the other hand he pulled one of the dusty sheets over the top of the cart.

'What are you doing?' she whispered.

'We can't get down the hall in time, and *I'm* not getting caught.'

Jamie wasn't looking forward to being discovered either, but every moment things got worse. Now the headlines would read: *Heirs of Malcomb's and S. & S. caught in a stock hamper while stealing hat.*

Before she could make any more objections, the echoing footsteps returned to the hall and were rapidly coming closer. Almost immediately she heard the second pair join the first, and the hamper moved as one of the guards brushed by it. Afraid the men might somehow see inside, through the canvas, Jamie grasped Tom's arm. That was when she realised she had left the hat, covered by her jacket, lying somewhere. She looked despairingly at Tom.

Then she let the worry over it drop away. She remembered putting it on a box, and the hat was covered by the jacket. The guards would never notice it with all the other clutter around. And if they did, she no longer cared. There was only so much she would do to save her pride, and she had done it. If she stayed on that platform for a year, it wasn't worth going through any more scares.

Tom had no idea what her expression implied. As he moved, trying to give her more room, he seemed to think she was uncomfortable. She was. Those hampers were made to hold almost everything, but two full grown people pretty well filled one. They lay in a tangle of arms and legs, and Jamie, half braced against Tom, could feel the wooden platform beneath the canvas as it bruised her hip and side.

At least Tom should be satisfied, she thought. She was trapped in his arms, but she doubted if he could enjoy the cramped position. The proximity of the guards would keep him from taking advantage of the situation. She looked up, showing him a smug expression, the best she could do, since she dared not speak. The guards were too close to risk even a whisper, she thought, though between the rattle of their lunch boxes and their conversation, a robber could have walked out with the whole store and they wouldn't have heard a thing.

And why did they have to pick that particular place to have their lunch—dinner or whatever they called it? She frowned at Tom, wondering if he had somehow engineered the whole thing. How—to books on seduction never mentioned canvas hampers—or did they? He was getting that gleam in his eye again.

'Don't you get any ideas, Jamie mouthed at him, reinforcing her order with a frown and a narrowing of the eyes, but she was too late. She leaned back against the canvas, but moving carefully, he crossed the six inches of space between their bodies. His eyes, still showing that devilish expression, seemed to hold her still as his lips closed on hers.

She felt herself emotionally lifted, swimming, swirling in a growing desire which was tempered but not erased by the danger of discovery. The danger and desire seemed to mingle together for a moment, each fanning the other as his lips kept moving over hers. Ever so slowly his arms crept around her, pulling her closer.

Cornered in that small space, and knowing she couldn't get away, she suddenly realised she had given up any thought of doing so. Willingly, travelling with his insistence, she allowed him to bring her body closer to his. Then the cart suddenly rocked.

Their faces inches part, they stared wide-eyed at each other, wondering if they were going to find themselves staring up at the security guards, who must have seen the tilting cart. Breathlessly they waited.

The headlines changed: *Heirs to Malcomb's and S. & S. caught making love in a stock hamper while stealing hat.*

At the table, not twenty feet away, one of the security guards had turned on a radio and both men were arguing over a sports score. There had been a pause in the conversation when the hamper rocked, but that could have been natural. Still, it was minutes before either Tom or Jamie relaxed.

The conversation between the two men went on as before. One, with a voice so deep he seemed to be croaking, was more voluble than the other, but as she listened, Jamie wondered what was wrong with him. His sentences were rambling and disjointed.

A moment or two later she didn't have time to worry about the guards. She had enough trouble with Tom. He was wearing a smug grin as his fingers played along the side of her cheek, daring her to stop him.

All romantic response had to be lost when even the slightest movement would give them away, she decided. Strange how the skin beneath his fingers didn't seem to realise that they could be discovered at any time. The thrills kept travelling along her cheek, working their way to her ear. His other arm, encircling her back, was partially trapped, but his hand slid along her side and hip, causing her flesh to quiver under his touch.

Enough of this, she thought. She tried to push him away.

'Just keep your mind on the job,' she whispered. 'No side issues.''

How had she dared speak? she wondered, but obviously the radio and the conversation at the table covered her. The argument over two professional hockey teams went on without pause.

'We got the hat,' Tom answered in a whisper, and brought his lips to hers again.

No, I'm not going to lose all sense, Jamie told herself. She needed leverage to get away from him, so she reached up, intending to catch hold of the metal frame. She missed the frame and brushed the sheet that covered them. A light sifting of dust came down.

Tom's amorous efforts came to an abrupt half as he drew back. His mouth opened as he sucked in breath in preparation for a sneeze. Jamie tensed, awaiting the inevitable.

The headline changed. *Heirs to Malcomb's and S. & S. caught sneezing and making love in a canvas hamper while stealing hat.* The paper would have to put out a larger edition!

With a tortured sigh his sneeze was aborted. Not one to be turned from his purpose, he started to kiss her again, but before his lips touched hers, Jamie was caught by silent gasps and put her hand up to her nose. She was not as successful as Tom. She suppressed the sound, but the aborted attempt set their hiding place rocking again.

No hope, she thought. Now the sheet had to be jerked away, they had to be discovered. But their luck seemed to be phenomenal. The gravel-voiced guard announced that their rest period was up.

'What's your hurry?' the other complained. 'By my watch, we still have five minutes.'

'Well, your watch is wrong, so let's go.'

Within two minutes the lunch boxes had been slammed shut, the radio turned off, and the footsteps receded down the corridor. Tom and Jamie suppressed their sneezing and climbed out of the hamper. At first her legs, cramped for so long, refused to obey her. When she stumbled, Tom reached out to help her, but she could tell he was none too steady himself.

'Let's get out of here,' he said as soon as her muscles were obeying her again. She grabbed the hat and covered it with the jacket. 'I hope I never come into this store again as long as I live!'

'What a way to talk!' Tom chided her. 'And I was thinking of having that hamper bronzed.'

'You can pick the strangest places to make a pass,' Jamie commented.

'You threw me out of your apartment—now you take me where you find me,' he retorted with a grin.

When they arrived at the side door, the waiting security guard nodded respectfully to Tom and unlocked the door. Outside the store, Jamie breathed deeply, feeling as if she could breathe again without the invisible restrictions of impending bars around her. But the feeling only lasted until they reached the warehouses. They retraced their course, back down the alley, in at the side door, through Malcomb's, stopping and peering around corners, making sure they stayed out of the path of the patrolling guards. Back in the S. & S. section, Jamie found a pair of scissors and clipped the Malcomb's price tag from the hat while Tom straightened the box.

She slipped it inside, put the lid on it and smiled at him. 'I feel as if I've travelled the world to end up in the same spot.'

'Next time, someone else can tell you how to run the belt,' said Tom. 'I'm too old for these dangerous missions.'

'Are you folks still here?' The security guard who had closed the platform doors had just come into the room and stood frowning. 'Where have you been? I didn't see you on my last round, Mr. Malcomb.'

'Oh, just checking up on some last-minute items for

Easter,' Tom said casually. He gave the elderly man a wide grin and a wink.

The guard was in a study for a moment and then his look turned sly. 'Want I should let you out?'

Jamie knew she was tired, but not how tired until the door of the warehouse had closed behind them. Only then did the meaning of Tom's grin and wink, and the guard's sly look, hit her. She stopped dead, glaring up at Tom Malcomb.

'Why did you do that?' she demanded. 'Do you have any idea what that man is thinking about us?'

He took her arm and propelled her towards the parking lot. 'I don't care what he believes—just as long as he doesn't think we were stealing hats.'

'But—but—' Jamie struggled against the tug on her arm until she caught the truth behind his remark. He had been as worried as she, and never once did he let it show. She walked at his side until they reached her car.

'Is that thing running okay now?' he asked as she unlocked the door.

'It's fine,' she said. His question meant he was going to see her on her way, not follow her home. She was partly relieved, but mostly disappointed. She hated to have the evening end so soon.

'Then I'll leave you—' he dragged out the words, as if hesitant to say them. 'And by the way, if I ever take to robbery as a career, I think you'd make a great accomplice.'

His arms encircled her, and she raised her lips to meet his kiss. For the first time she let her feelings go. Her need for him filled her, and she clung to him, wanting to keep him with her. Suddenly a sense of loss as if she were left alone seemed to be inconsolable. When they parted she was shaken, and Tom's breathing seemed a little ragged.

Jamie gave way to the desire to run her fingers down

the line of his cheek and jaw. She covered her growing feelings with a light remark and turned towards the car.

'Somehow, swiping hats with anyone else just wouldn't have been the same,' she said as she opened the door of the Volkswagen.

'In a stock hamper?' George Stone looked up from his baked potato. He and Abel were in Stone & Stone again for lunch, since Abel's doctor, who was also his cousin and a stockholder in Malcomb's, had talked with the company chef.

Abel ignored the question until he had finished his lobster Thermidor. With a sigh of ecstasy, he sipped the white wine he had smuggled into the S. & S. executive dining room.

'In a stock hamper,' he finally confirmed. 'And that's a new one on me.'

George frowned, his mouth open as if to speak, but sheer incredulity kept his words back at first. His hand with his fork was half raised as he jabbed the air. Finally the words came out.

'Why were they over there after store hours, and why in a hamper?'

'Search me,' shrugged Abel, and took a forkful of cauliflower with hollandaise sauce. 'Think I'll get my chef to give yours a recipe for hollandaise.'

'Keep your recipe, and go on with the story,' George demanded.

'Got no story,' Abel said, 'just a lot of questions. Frog—you know Frog, he quits here and comes to us—'

'Yeah—but stop getting off the track.'

'You really ought to take that recipe—'

'One more word about that sauce, and you can go back to your rabbit food! Now get back to that stock hamper!'

'Don't be so impatient, you can't enjoy anything that way—okay, okay, all I know is what Frog told me. Seems he saw Tom and "this young woman", as he called her, sidling around in the service corridors after hours. He didn't figure it was any of his business to start asking Tom questions.'

'I would.'

Abel savoured a bite of potatoes au gratin before going on with his story.

'You're not an employee. Frog came to me because he thought if Tom was fooling around with a stock clerk, I should do something about it—you know these characters who have been around here from the year one. They think Tom's as much their son as mine, but I'm the one that should keep him in line.'

'Much you could do about it if he was having an affair,' George grunted.

'Frog said he couldn't figure out where they disappeared to, so imagine his surprise, when he was on his supper break, and he sees this cart start rocking back and forth. He nearly swallowed a chicken bone.'

George shook his head. 'They wouldn't have been in a cart. Not together—why would they?'

'I asked Frog if he was sure they were both in there. According to him there were too many elbows and knees poking the canvas sides for it to be one person. He was in a devil of a fix. Another guard was with him—'

'Did the other one see them? We don't want any talk.' George looked upset.

'Not according to Frog. Seems the other guy's back was to the hamper, and Frog talked till he was hoarse, and got the other guard away. Then, still not sure it was them, he hid and watched them leave. It was Tom and the girl, all right. He went back, and there wasn't but one empty, he said.'

'In a stock hamper!' George shook his head again.

'All I can say is, Tom has developed some new talents.'

'I'll say he has—they must be unique!'

'Don't get your virtue outraged, what could have happened? There's no room, and that's not what I had in mind anyway,' Abel grinned. 'The next morning he was eating his breakfast and whistling at the same time. Looks like things are moving along according to plan.'

'Whatever happened, it's got Jamie all upset,' said George. 'One thing I never thought of—she feels she's lying to people by calling herself Stevens. It's Tom she's got in mind, of course.'

'Well, tell her the truth,' Abel said easily. 'Tell her Tom knows. He can't say anything—he gave his word he wouldn't.'

'If I admit I lied, she won't stick with the bargain.'

'George, you're an underhanded, double-dealing scoundrel!'

'Yeah,' the president of the board of Stone & Stone grinned complacently. Suddenly he leaned over, and with his fork took a small portion of the cauliflower with hollandaise. He tasted it thoughtfully. 'There's nothing wrong with that sauce. You're only trying to justify what you pay that cook of yours.'

'Chef,' Abel corrected him, 'and your taste is in your feet.' He took another sip of his wine and put the glass down with a sigh. 'But I sure would like to know what they were doing in that hamper.'

'Abel—' George pushed away his lunch, frowning, 'if Tom was whistling and eating at the same time, I don't think we want to know—at least not for sure.'

CHAPTER SIX

In your Easter bonnet, with all the frills upon it, the words sang in Jamie's head as she logged in the last shipment on the platform. She looked up at the clock—eleven-thirty, and there were no trucks in the street, no blasting air horns blowing their impatience, no roaring engines. The rush of shipments seemed to be over for a while. The spring fashions that had been clogging the receiving platform for weeks, the merchandise for the spring sales had arrived. From other parts of the city the new life in the budding trees, early flowers and the general feeling of spring was wafting itself over the bleak warehouse area of town.

Was it the season, or was there really a freshness to the old buildings and the cobblestoned streets? Or was it, Jamie wondered, because of her own spirits? She had been treading that spring air ever since Wednesday night after she and Tom had replaced the hat.

I think you'd make a great accomplice, he had said. Every time those words echoed in her mind, she gave them a new and different meaning. Did he? she wondered.

And yet the thought threw her into the doldrums. He might help her replace a hat, but basically he was honest and above board. What would his reaction be when he discovered the truth? He'd know her for a liar—pretending to be something she wasn't and not trusting him enough to tell him the truth. But she had given her word to Uncle George, and she couldn't break that either, could she?

Everything will work out, she told herself for the

umpteenth time in two days. Somehow I'll make him understand I was caught between a rock and a hard place. But could she? She would, she insisted. She must.

As if just thinking about him was enough to call him, she glanced towards, the door that led into Malcomb's warehouse, and saw him as he appeared. He was walking by the door, but he stopped and looked in her direction. When he spotted her, he reached up, carefully adjusted an invisible hat and disappeared with a smile.

Jamie chuckled. 'In your Easter bonnet,' she sang softly as she turned back towards the receiving office cubicle. She was just approaching the door when she saw Velma at the opening where the conveyor system went through the wall and into the pricing area. The bleached blonde was motioning her towards the ladies' lounge.

Jamie stepped into the office, put her clipboard on the desk and started across the platform, thinking Velma wanted to gossip or perhaps go to lunch early. She didn't want to make a practice of leaving the platform to Freddy and Carl, but at the moment she was at a loose end.

But when she went into the lounge, all idea of gossip was dispelled by the tight look on Velma's face. Llewellyn was sitting on the vinyl couch, crying.

'What's wrong?' asked Jamie.

'We've got trouble,' Velma said. 'We need help, but you've got to promise not to say a word about it.'

'I'll do what I can—' Jamie hesitated. She was reluctant about giving her word when she didn't know what was involved.

'If they find out, I'll be arrested,' Llewellyn sobbed.

'Stop saying that!' Velma snapped at the weeping girl. 'You keep talking that way and someone will believe you should be!' She turned to Jamie, shaking her head. 'She ought to be fired. Always mooning over that Rick, so busy watching him she can't keep her mind on her job. I've warned her—'

'You still haven't told me what's wrong,' Jamie broke in.

'She's responsible for twenty-one,' said Velma, expecting that to answer all Jamie's questions. 'She knows she should be damn careful with that jewellery.'

Jamie's adrenalin started pumping again. She felt a cold wash go through her. 'What happened?'

'I don't know,' Llewellyn muttered, her voice trembling. 'It was all there, and then it was all gone!'

'It has to be upstairs, mixed in with another shipment,' Velma said, suddenly staring at Jamie as if she suddenly distrusted her. The look quickly faded. Still, her tone was belligerent, defensive. 'Llewellyn may be an idiot, but she's certainly no thief—and neither are the rest of my people.'

'I'm sure of that,' Jamie said quickly. And wanting to bring hope to a desperate situation, she added, 'It shouldn't be too hard to find—we can just check the carts Llewellyn has been loading. The jewellery probably got hooked on to a dress or something.'

'No,' said Velma, shaking her head. 'She doesn't take it out of the boxes, she just holds it for the store shuttle.'

'Then it should be even easier to find,' Jamie said confidently. 'We'll just have to go upstairs and search.'

Velma's face softened. 'That's why we needed you. We were hoping you'd ask us to go up with you to check on a shipment—something one of the buyers wanted— we can't let Hugh Belmont know. I've had several real dingbats lately. He fired one of my girls not long ago, not that she didn't deserve it; but he's watching my department.'

What happened to honesty and straight dealing? Jamie wondered as she hurried back to her office and checked several orders, choosing one that was unlikely to be questioned. Then she skipped in to see Hugh, telling him she was going upstairs to check an order for a buyer. He seemed to think nothing of her taking Velma, head of the pricing section, and Llewellyn, since this particular order would have passed through her section.

But once on the third floor, she let Velma organise the search. '. . . And for heaven's sake, Llewellyn, keep that man off your mind long enough to pay attention,' she finished.

Jamie felt for the girl, whose shoulders were bowed under the load of her fear. A few weeks ago she would have taken an entirely different attitude about the lost jewellery. Her father had drilled it into her head that an inefficient employee was poison to the company, and a responsible person worried about the business first, for the sake of the good employees on the staff as well as the profit sheet.

But that had been before she had spent days sharing a lunch table with Llewellyn, seeing her suffering over her ill-starred love affair. She saw in it a parallel of her own feelings about Tom Malcomb. And Velma had been right—Llewellyn might have her mind somewhere else, but she certainly wasn't dishonest. In the rush of handling a lot of shipments, anything could be misplaced. It was just unfortunate that this one was particularly valuable. The penalty expected by Velma and the girl was too severe for the intention.

At twelve-thirty, they had been searching for almost an hour. Jamie straightened, twisting her shoulders to relieve the strain of bending over the lower shelves of an open cart, and looked across the way at Llewellyn.

'Is it your responsibility to unpack and sort everything that comes in?'

'I like that!' Velma grunted from where she was checking carts that held a shipment of blankets. 'The rest of us don't sit around twiddling our thumbs!'

For another ten minutes they kept looking. Then Jamie was struck with a thought that caused her knees to weaken. She stood up, feeling the coolness of her face as the blood seemed to drain away.

'Velma!' she called to the pricing supervisor. 'Could those little boxes get caught up with the trash?'

'Oh, my God!' Velma whirled around, staring at Llewellyn. The tall thin girl was the only calm one.

She shook her head resolutely. 'No way,' she said, positive for the first time since they had begun the search. 'Iris and I go through each other's trash before we load it in a bin. Besides, I always put twenty-one right in a store bin. I still think I switched boxes and piled something else on top of it.'

'Twenty-one?' Hugh Belmont's voice crossed the room like a fast glacier, freezing the three girls in its path.

For a moment Jamie stood perfectly still, not sure what to do. Llewellyn had lost the jewellery, but Jamie had been the one to deliberately lie to the warehouse manager. She could just hear her uncle when he learned she had been fired!

Llewellyn was the first to move. She had been emotionally all to pieces in the ladies' lounge, but faced with the worst, she pulled on hidden reserves. In a voice far from steady, she explained what had happened, and why they were searching.

'It was just a mistake, Hugh,' said Velma, stepping forward. Most of her bravado had disappeared. He was, after all, her boss, and she was also covering a problem that could have serious consequences.

Jamie stood watching the interplay of emotions among the other three. She couldn't really blame Hugh for his frozen face. He was just one in a cabin. His mind was probably running amok with the consequences if that jewellery wasn't found. He'd been with the store for years, and probably had dreams of promotions leading up to what, a vice-presidency? Suddenly she saw the unimportance of what her uncle thought, versus what those three people faced.

While she watched she saw his face mirror all the things she had been thinking. Anger, desperation and distrust were all in his reactions.

'*Lost?*' he glared at Llewellyn, his tone too broadly disbelieving not to have some conscious force behind it.

Jamie winced as the poor girl started to tremble.

'That's the only answer, Hugh,' Vera was trying to placate him, but she was stopped by a withering glare.

'Maybe you'll tell me,' he turned on her, 'why it had to be department twenty-one? We get other small shipments, but nothing else as valuable; and nothing else was lost, was it?'

Jamie, looking on from what she recognised to be her relatively impervious position, felt she should stay out of the argument. But Llewellyn was torn apart by her fear. Hugh's attitude towards the unfortunate girl brought her anger to a scalding temperature.

'If that's true, it's surprising,' Jamie snapped. 'And if this is the first time those little boxes have gone astray, I'd be surprised!'

All three people turned and stared at her, but she wasn't through. She was a Stone, and if the fact was hidden, the attitude was fast coming to the surface. 'They don't belong back there with so much bulk merchandise, and even if they did, Llewellyn wouldn't deliberately misroute them. She's no thief. I think *your* responsibility to the warehouse should be to help us find those darn boxes, not to call a good employee a thief!'

That was it, he'd fire her, but if he did, what did she have to lose? She'd just tell him who she was and order him to help look. She stood, fists clenched, waiting for his reaction. When it came, she was floored. He looked as if he wanted to retort in kind, and then he swallowed noisily.

'You're right, of course, Miss Ston—Miss Stevens.' He turned to Llewellyn. 'Where have you looked?'

Jamie was momentarily stunned. Hugh knew who she was! Since his information hadn't come from her, her uncle must have been the culprit with the loose lips. Accidentally or deliberately? she wondered. Deliberately, because he wanted to make sure nothing happened to her, she supposed.

Across a twenty-foot space, Jamie and Velma stared at each other. Llewellyn was too occupied with her problem to catch the slip in names. She was so relieved not to be immediately fired that she was hastily showing Hugh where they had searched. Velma was a lot sharper; she looked as if she had been betrayed.

'Let's have lunch,' said Jamie. 'If those boxes are here, they won't be going anywhere for an hour.'

'No, they won't,' Velma answered, but her voice was formal. Gone was all the companionable warmth Jamie had been accustomed to hearing.

Side by side they rode the elevator, went into the lounge to wash their hands and came out to cross the street. Not until they were sitting at a table in the almost empty cafeteria did Jamie bring up the subject that was bothering both of them.

'Everyone has to work,' she said quietly.

'Not everybody,' answered Velma, not raising her eyes from her plate.

Jamie knew what the older woman meant. Her salary went to support herself and her granddaughter; Jamie's millions would keep her in goodies all her life without any effort on her part.

'They have to work at something, even if it's nothing but boredom,' she contradicted. 'Who I am is not the point—it's because you didn't know, isn't it?'

The importance of Velma's answer loomed over Jamie's head like a cloud. Her reaction would be a forewarning of what to expect from Tom when he found out, she decided. She waited with both impatience and dread while Velma idly stirred her iced tea. When she met Jamie's eyes, Jamie could see confusion and pain.

'We thought you were one of us—I trusted you with Llewellyn's secret,' she said. 'The remarks Iris made about Tom Malcomb—the cracks about the big shots on the top floor of the store—'

'I didn't split on Llewellyn,' Jamie said lamely. She had been prepared for Velma to be angry, but not hurt. That hadn't been on her list of expected reactions.

There was no reason why she should explain to the supervisor of the pricing department why she was in a warehouse that was forty-per cent hers, but she knew she wanted to. She wanted this new friend to understand. In some way, she thought later, it was as if she was explaining it to Tom.

'. . . So, you see, it wasn't to fool anyone. I'm not spying, it's just that Uncle George wanted me to have the total experience, not some token job—'

'Hugh knew,' said Velma, making all Jamie's explanations sound like so much hot air.

'But *I* wasn't aware of it,' Jamie said. She had pushed that fact back in her mind, feeling it could wait until she had straightened out the misunderstanding between herself and Velma.

'And I guess Tom Malcomb knows,' said Velma. She was still a little formal, keeping her eyes carefully averted from Jamie, but one short glance at her companion caused all Velma's new reserve to fall away.

'Honey, he *does* know?'

Jamie shook her head. 'Who would tell him? I can't, I gave my word not to let it out. Hugh Belmont just slipped up; he wouldn't deliberately mention it. I'm sure

Uncle George swore him to secrecy. Even if Uncle George can't be trusted to keep it quiet, you can be sure he threatened Hugh with Lower Slobovia.'

Velma shook her head, the male/female wisdom of the ages in her eyes. She pushed away her plate and crossed her arms on the table, leaning forward to give Jamie the benefit of that knowledge.

'Sweetie, have you ever heard of the male ego? I don't think anyone ever figured out what keeps it going, but Lord help the woman who dents it. My second husband, Harry—no, he was the third—skip Harry. Just believe me, honey, you can't keep fooling him and expect him to take it with a smile on his face.'

Jamie braced her chin in her hand. She was relieved that Velma was over her first shock, and they were still friends. She would have felt lighthearted if she could be sure Tom would accept the truth as easily, but she couldn't depend upon that. Not even the blonde, self-appointed bombshell thought so.

'Velma, you're warning me about something, I know. Now what do I do about it? And don't suggest telling him yourself.'

'If it was me, I'd let someone tell him and shake the dust of this place right off my feet,' said Velma. 'With you who you are, it's just plain silly for you to be here.'

'No, Velma, this is just where I should be,' Jamie countered. 'I don't have to keep my word to Uncle George—he broke the bargain—but I've got to stay. I'm beginning to see a different world, one I need to understand.' She was thinking of Llewellyn, and what her attitude about the lost jewellery would have been if she had travelled straight from Arizona to the seventh floor and the administrative offices.

The incident on the third floor of the warehouse had given her her first inkling of the compromises people had to make in their lives and their principles to keep their jobs and provide for their families. She had come within an inch of not speaking up for Llewellyn, and her only reason had been to save herself embarrassment with her uncle. Deep within her, she knew no one in the company could cause her more than a temporary discomfort.

But the situation had been different for Hugh, who could see a career draining away with the loss of that jewellery. Llewellyn could see disgrace, and Velma, for her part, could have lost her livelihood for a time. She still had only an inkling of how much pressure the average worker, dependent upon that weekly pay cheque and the good opinion of his superiors, could sustain. What else would she learn, and what would she miss if she left now? How much damage could she do by her ignorance? She shook her head stubbornly.

'I took the job because of Uncle George, but I'm keeping it, at least for the present, for myself and the company.'

'Honey, if I had a hunk like that caught on my line, I'd forget all about companies and offices and warehouses, and just say "Sweetie, I'm all yours!"'

Jamie smiled, wishing she could see the situation in that light. She was saved from trying to explain to Velma what the woman would never understand by the arrival of Llewellyn. The girl's face was wreathed in smiles.

'We found them,' she said, putting her tray on the table. 'In a store flat of pillowcases, of all things! I remember now just what happened. I laid the first of the pillowcases on top of the tray, meaning to put them somewhere else, and I forgot. Then I just picked up the tray and put it on the cart.' She looked over at Jamie, smiling shyly. 'Thank you for speaking up for me. Oh, I was afraid of what Mr Belmont would say to you—he could have fired you, you know. I'm your friend for life after what you did for me!'

As Llewellyn turned her attention to her late lunch, Jamie and Velma exchanged a conspiratorial look. Obviously the girl, so upset over her own problems, had missed Hugh's slip.

Jamie arrived back on the platform in time to log in two shipments and free Carl to run the belt. When she was finished she went into the office and started work on her daily report. Usually she was forced to wait until the large doors on the receiving bays were closed before she had time to begin it, but in less than half an hour she had it current to the moment, and there was nothing left to do but add up the number of shipments and list the totals.

She sat staring out at the featureless concrete plantform, rendered even more uninteresting because Carl and Freddy had swept it thoroughly. Outside Hugh's office were a dozen large cartons containing lawn furniture left on their platform. The carrier was due back to pick them up and take them on to the bulk warehouse that handled furniture and other bulk merchandise. But Jamie's mind was not on shipments; she was too interested in her day's experience. Just how was she going to use what she had learned? she wondered. She had given her word to her uncle, but as part of a bargain he had destroyed by letting Hugh Belmont know who she was. By rights, she could walk off the job and straight into the main store. She was free of the warehouse if she wanted to be.

She wasn't walking off; there were too many things college and her father had omitted from her education. But she was free to tell Tom the truth, she decided. She would insist he keep her secret. Since she had begun the job as Jamie Stevens, she would stay Jamie Stevens possibly for more than the original time of six months, though with luck she would move into other departments, widening her experience. Her uncle, for all his sneaking ways, had been right about what she could learn.

Tom Malcomb would have to be told, she thought. She would take care of that at the first opportunity. She'd just march right up to him and—what? Did she just hold out her hand and say, 'Have we met? I'm Jamie Stone, your competitor.' That would go over like a lead balloon.

Possibly she could invite him over for dinner—and tell him the story of the prince and the pauper? That didn't quite fit the circumstances, either.

There would be a way, she decided. As soon as she found him alone, she would tell him. She became aware of a dry, woody taste in her mouth and gazed balefully at the pencil she had been chewing. The shiny yellow paint was chipped, the wood dented with teeth marks. Deciding Stone & Stone could survive the waste of one pencil, she dropped it in the waste box beside her desk.

As she straightened in her chair, she noticed Carl and Freddy. Their attitudes so closely resembled her and Tom's movements of the night before that she was intrigued. Carl was pressed against the wall separating the S. & S. warehouse from Malcomb's. Freddy's pale blond head appeared as he sheltered behind the large cartons of lawn furniture. As she watched, one of the workers from Malcomb's appeared briefly in the doorway and shot a missile at Carl by means of a rubber band. She watched the glitter as an object sailed through the air. It missed its target and came down on the concrete outside her office. When it slid to a stop just outside her office door, she saw it was a paper clip.

That decided the issue for Freddy. He turned and pelted towards the office where Jamie sat, watching. Instinctively, she knew his mission. She was not playing the part of the company executive, so it was no part of her job to make sure supplies were used properly. She reached behind her and took two boxes of clips from the small supply cabinet. As Freddy slid on the concrete floor, using his hold on the door-jamb to fling himself into the office, she tossed several thick rubber bands at him.

'Your weapons and ammunition,' she slid the small cardboard boxes across the desk. 'Your mission is to uphold the honour of good old S. & S.'

'Then you'd better help us, because we're outnumbered,' Freddy answered as he pocketed his artillery.

Out on the platform, Carl had been forced back by the Malcomb's employees until he had taken shelter behind the boxes of lawn furniture. One of the enemy was actually inside S. & S., advancing while his buddies covered him.

'We can't allow that,' muttered Jamie, getting into the spirit of the game. She reached for another box of clips and another thick rubber band and stepped out on the platform, watching the battle. For a moment she considered joining Freddy and Carl, but better strategy was needed. She turned in the other direction and knelt at the edge of the truck bay, easing her four-feet drop to the floor below. Out on the sidewalk, she hurried up the street past the terra-cotta drainpipe that was the only visible outside boundary between S. & S. and Malcomb's. Quietly she climbed up on to the Malcomb's platform and into enemy territory, just in time to see the last of the combatants slipping through the door into the S. & S. section. But as she walked quietly to the door, she was beginning to regret her decision. What would be the result of her game playing when everyone finally knew who she was? Would the memory of her taking part in childish games lead to a laxity on the part of the employees? Would she be undermining the authority of managers like Hugh Belmont?

She stood frowning, thinking about the result, and for

the first time realised the drawbacks of her situation. She was, she knew, responsible to the company to maintain a certain image, even as Jamie Stevens, because later everyone would know about the deception. But she *wanted* to let fly with her rubber band and score a hit on one of the Malcomb's employees. While she was trying to justify her desire to join the game, the decision was taken away from her. Iris and Llewellyn strolled out on the platform, and were immediately enlisted in the war. Now the opponents were fairly matched in numbers. There was no legitimate place for her.

Jamie sighed, partly relieved that the decision had been taken away from her, and partly because she regretted waiting too long before acting.

'S-sst!' Jamie looked around to locate the hiss and saw Tom standing in the dimness of a hallway that gave access to the back of the warehouse. He waved, gesturing her over, so she walked in his direction. Reluctantly, she reminded herself that she was committed to telling him her identity, but she thought she would have had more time to plan what she would say.

As she approached the hall, close enough for his low voice to be heard, he pointed to the door that led into her area.

'Who's winning?'

'Since Malcomb's is on our turf, I guess you are,' she said, still a little disgruntled that she was not part of the action. 'Go take a look.'

'Oh, I can't do that,' Tom answered, as if surprised that she would suggest such a thing. 'As manager I'm also sheriff, responsible for maintaining law and order. But what I don't see doesn't hurt anyone—at least, not on a slow day like this.'

Jamie nodded, watching him as he looked towards the doorway, listening for the sounds of the game. His face was slightly wistful as they heard a squeal from Iris and one of the boys congratulating another on a hit.

So he felt hemmed in by his position too, she thought, and sympathised. She remembered he had said as much that night in his office in the store, when he said the job itself was a trap. She knew now just what he meant, and she wanted to tell him so.

Perfect! That was exactly the opening she needed to put an end to her deception. From expressing her sympathy for his position, she could lead into her feelings, and then explain why she was on the receiving platform. She was just forming the words for her opening spiel when a shout came from the doorway and three of the Malcomb's battle squad were forced back into their own warehouse.

Tom grabbed her arm and pulled her back into the hall where they could see the action without being observed. But if they were to appear unaware of the paper clip war, they couldn't remain where they were. Two of the retreating forces dashed for the shelter of the hall, causing Jamie and Tom to sprint for an intersection some twenty feet down the corridor.

They had just turned the corner, Tom looking back to see the action and Jamie trying to peer around his broad shoulders, when the S. & S. attack force drove the Malcomb's people deeper into the building. The general retreat had started down the hall, so Jamie and Tom moved back to stay out of the way. Still not wanting to be seen, Jamie grabbed the handle of the door at the end and opened it. The door was unmarked. She assumed she was heading further into the warehouse, and dashed right in. She paused just inside the door, realising she had led them into a closet where brooms, mops, and other cleaning supplies were stored.

'Oops, dead end,' she said, but by that time Tom was right behind her and had closed the door, leaving them in complete darkness.

'Hey, this is a closet,' Jamie complained.

'There's a very special something about you.' Tom's voice, coming out of the darkness, was low and sensual. Jamie remembered the sound of it when they were wandering in the darkness the night they had exchanged the hats. Strange, she thought, but without those laughing eyes to give it humour, his voice was dangerously provocative.

'You do manage to get us alone together, and in the most interesting places,' he continued.

For a moment Jamie mistrusted her understanding of his remark. He certainly didn't think she had deliberately led them into that closet—he certainly sounded as if he did. Of all the nerve! She guessed he considered the trip through the warehouse and the scuffle in the hamper her idea too. She wasn't taking that.

'Wait a minute, don't blame this on me,' she countered. 'You were the one who couldn't be seen watching. I'm just a warehouse clerk, and not responsible for the rest of the crew. And turn on the light.' Now why had she said that? She had it all planned to tell him the truth, and she had ruined the mood.

'There's no light. This room was never wired, and you certainly can't blame it on me,' he answered softly, his breath moving the hair on the top of her head as they stood close together in the cramped quarters. 'If I had chosen the escape route, I certainly wouldn't have led you into a closet. I don't have that much imagination.'

Jamie turned around to face him. In the complete darkness her action was totally useless, but she lacked experience in fighting with her back turned to her opponent.

'I didn't know it was a closet,' she insisted, aware that he was teasing her, and her protests would make no impression. Still she felt it necessary to let him know she had not manoeuvred him into anything.

'Well, for future reference, in case you want to lead me back here, I'll explain—this is a broom closet. We can have it all to ourselves for the next hour and a half, but—'

Jamie decided she'd been wrong about the darkness, or maybe the red she was seeing came from inside her.

'You open that door!' she demanded, thinking for one foolish moment that she should scream the building down. But common sense took over immediately, warning her she could never do that. The talk wouldn't stop with the warehouse or the stores. It would be all over town in twenty-four hours.

'Let's not do that,' his voice was soothing. 'We'll mess up all the fun. Next week those characters have to be on the ball every minute. We're getting the big shots from several stores touring the warehouses. They would have been here today, but something went wrong with the arrangements.'

'Well, that's just too bad—now get us out of this closet,' Jamie demanded again, wishing suddenly that she had joined the game on the platform. Being shot at with a rubber band and a paper clip was a lot less dangerous than contemplating murder.

'But I like it in here,' said Tom. The sensual vibrations in his voice increased tenfold, and she felt his breath on her forehead as he stepped closer.

Angry with him for his assumption that she had led him into their embarrassing position, and in no mood for romance, Jamie stepped back—and suppressed a scream as her neck came up against something sharp. She felt as if she were being nipped by a thousand little mouths. With her arms outspread to keep from colliding with some other object, she leapt forward, right into Tom's arms.

'I like it better and better,' he murmured as she clutched him in her fright.

Her anger was submerged under her fear, and for a moment she clung to him, just glad he was there to protect her. But from what?

'Something bit my neck,' she said, not sure herself whether she was explaining her sudden change of attitude, or whether she expected him to do something about it.

'Lucky something,' murmured Tom, and his fingers created a sensual path as they moved up her back to move experimentally along the exposed skin of her neck. 'Does that hurt?'

'No, it—they—whatever it was didn't break the skin,' she acknowledged. If it had been an insect she would have felt a sting, she realised. Maybe she hadn't really been bitten, but she had thought so at the time. If she could see what she had backed into, she would feel much safer. She wouldn't be clinging to him in this outrageous way.

'Yes, some things have all the luck,' Tom said. She felt him move, his head brush hers as his lips came to rest on the side of her neck. 'I'll just kiss away the hurt.'

No, you won't, she tried to say, but his mouth, warm and tantalising, was moving over her skin, sending shivers of desire through her body. As if working without her knowledge, her arms tightened around him, revelling in their hold on his powerful, muscular back. Her fingers drew a path across his shoulders and disturbed the short hair on the back of his neck, causing him to shiver.

When his mouth travelled from her throat, across her jaw, and found her lips, an unbidden moan of pleasure escaped her lips and was reduced to a whimper of pleasure. His was the kiss out of a dream, that netherland where woman went within her heart to wonder and to savour what it meant to be cherished and adored. His lips, tender and gentle at first, gradually became more insistent; neither demanding nor begging, but requesting, letting her know what it meant to be needed and to know the power and the burden of being loved.

She would have fought an arrogant assumption that she must dissolve into jelly at his masculinity. Instead, she found herself giving out of a need to give, making the choice he allowed her. She pressed closer to him, delighting in the right to express the hunger that he caused to grow within her.

When his lips freed hers and brushed across her cheek, kissing her temples, her earlobe, the desire building in her threatened not to be contained. She was breathless, panting with her emotion. His arms eased their tight embrace, but as she stepped back slightly she remembered her scare in the dark and moved towards him again, her hands reaching for his shoulders.

Instead of touching Tom, her hand brushed the wall and came to rest on what was unmistakably a light switch. She flipped it on.

Tom frowned and squinted against the sudden flood of light, but Jamie's scowl was less because of the sharp illumination. She had a second reason.

'No light, huh?' she spat at him. Remembering her fear, she looked over her shoulder and saw what had given her the fright. Against the back wall were several wide, wooden-headed brooms, and one was upended. She had backed into the stiff bristles. She glared at him, her eyes sparkling with renewed anger.

'You *knew* that was a broom!' she accused.

His eyes were full of laughter as he shrugged. 'Well, it *is* a broom closet.'

'Oh—' Jamie spluttered for a moment before she could get her words around her anger. 'You—you animal!'

His answer was to give a low growl and step in her direction. She decided to take immediate action against that and punched him in the stomach with one small fist. Her blow had carried very little force, and when he bent forward, exaggerating a non-existent pain, she became madder than ever.

'You stay away from me!' she ordered. 'I thought I was wrong about you, but my first impression of you was right—no, it wasn't—' She pushed by him to throw open the door. She stepped out into the hall and had started up the corridor before she realised she had not had her say and stopped, turning to face him.

'I thought you were looking for—what did that old country and Western song say?—a back street affair—'

She saw him pause in the act of stepping out of the closet after turning off the light, but she was too angry to worry about his expression.

'Now wait a minute—' he said, but she cut him off. 'But after your back halls, warehouses, hampers and closets, I think I'd find a back street a relief!'

Jamie turned again and ran down the hall. She could hear steps behind her, but once she was on the platform of Malcomb's, she knew he would not follow. He could not be seen chasing a warehouse clerk—not the great Tom Malcomb.

CHAPTER SEVEN

As Jamie strode back across the Malcomb's platform, went through the door and headed for her cubicle of an office, she encountered Hugh Belmont. After a glance at her expression, he looked wary and hesitant.

Maybe there would be some benefit in his knowing who she was after all, Jamie thought. She was independent of his approval, and right then that suited her mood.

'I'm caught up except for finalising the report,' she said briskly. 'Carl and Freddy can handle any last-minute deliveries.' If he misunderstood her intention to leave for the day, he lacked understanding, she thought.

Twenty minutes later, when she entered her apartment, she was still seething over Tom's trick in the closet. She threw her jacket and bag on the bed and strode into the bathroom, turning on the taps for a hot bath. Feeling the need for a little extra luxury, she loaded the water with scented bubble bath and closed the sliding glass doors to keep the heat of the water from invading the rest of the room.

'You asked for it,' she snarled at her reflection in the mirror as she stripped for her bath. 'You knew what he was, the way he behaved, you broke your rules— remember you had rules?' She jerked off her shirt and bra and turned to frown at her reflection again. Why did the eyes in the mirror seem to be laughing at her?

'Why did you listen when he told you there was no light switch in that closet?' she demanded of the reflection. 'Were you stupid enough to think they'd put in half

125

a million dollars' worth of equipment and not wire a closet?'

Is that what you're really *arguing about?* the reflection seemed to ask.

'You're darned right!' Jamie snapped back, but she busied herself with removing her shoes, jeans and panties and refused to look at the reflection again. When she sat down in her bath, the bubbles were up to her nose. She batted them away by the handful until she was in a little valley of perfumed clouds and leaned back, letting the hot water help relieve the tensions that had knotted her muscles.

As she relaxed physically, her emotions calmed. She *had* opened the door of the broom closet, she reasoned. Now she could smile at the way she had dashed in pell-mell, so intent on getting away from the paper clip war that she had taken no time to consider. But *he* was the one who allowed her to be frightened and refused to admit there was a light, she argued, frowning again.

But he *had* protected her, even if it was only from a broom. The frown dissolved into a smile of sensuous memory as she remembered the comfort of his arms. Even in the darkness she had felt safe and secure, but those feelings had been overridden by sensations so intense, so fiery, even the warmth of the water cooled in comparison. His kiss, so different from any in her admittedly limited experience, still seemed to linger on her lips. She shivered with pleasure as she wondered what would have happened if she had not found that light switch. That brought back the memory of his duplicity, and she sat up abruptly.

'Oh, that *man!*' she exclaimed, and took a swing at a mountain of bubbles. With a sigh of exasperation, she watched as they floated through the opening and settled on the clean, shining floor of the bathroom. In her upset, she had forgotten to close the sliding glass door.

An hour and a half later, she slipped into a lounging robe after washing and drying her hair and cleaning the bathroom of what seemed like acres of stubborn bubbles. She had, in the process, made another rule. Tom Malcomb was going to stay out of her life, and out of her mind. She was not going to blame him for anything that had happened, but neither was she going to allow anything else to upset her plans. He was still the competition, and planned or not, he was keeping her mind off her business. She was going to forget him.

She picked up a book and settled in a chair in the living-room of the small apartment, but by the tenth page she was finding the opinions of a supposed genius in economics as dry as dust.

'What the world needs is for instructors to get out in it before they start expounding theories,' she said aloud. Before she could elaborate to herself on that idea, the doorbell rang.

Book still in her hand, she crossed the room and opened the door. Velma stood outside, Jamie's blue sweater over her arm, and a white envelope in her hand.

'Special messenger service, sweetie.'

'Well—er—hi,' said Jamie, too confused to make sense even to herself. As she stared at the blonde woman, she knew part of her problem was disappointment. Since only her uncle and Tom Malcomb knew where she lived, she had expected Tom to be standing in the hall. As she stood, one hand on the door, she was jerked out of her thoughts by Velma's expression of discomfort. Aware that she was not making Velma feel welcome, Jamie tried to undo the impression her surprise and confusion had made.

'Come in—so good of you to come by—you brought my sweater—thank you so much—' She sounded patronising. With a sinking heart she saw Velma's face close. When the pricing supervisor held out the sweater and envelope without a word, Jamie reached out, caught her arm and pulled her into the apartment.

'Don't mind me, I've flipped my noodle completely today,' she said by way of apology. 'I seem to have lost what little sense I had.'

Velma nodded sagely and relaxed. 'You and Tom have had a doozy of a fight!'

Jamie felt her jaw drop. Weakly, she reached for the still open door, holding on to it for stability.

'Don't tell me we were overheard!'

Velma turned to lay the sweater on the arm of a chair. 'Not that I know of, but honey, you're talking to an old warhorse in the game of love. When you left so abruptly, after being in the Malcomb's warehouse, and he stalked around for an hour before talking Hugh into letting me leave early to bring you your sweater, I knew something was up. So it was no surprise to me, I can tell you, when he met me in the parking lot and gave me this love note.' She held out the letter.

'Love note?' Jamie queried with some suspicion.

'Dearie, I broke my cardinal rule of steaming open whatever comes into my hands. I didn't have to look—it glows with an apology.'

Jamie gestured for Velma to take a seat and opened the long white envelope with trembling fingers. Her last rule was fading from her mind as she read the missive.

Memo to all broom closet fugitives:

Very few good restaurants located on back streets. Best substitute, an old steamboat on canal by river. Does that qualify?

Reservation for eight. Sea-going crow the specialty of the house.

T. M.

'He's crazy,' laughed Jamie, completely forgetting her newest resolution. 'Crazy as a loon!'

'So was my fourth husband,' said Velma. 'He was always doing crazy, wild things. That's fatal, you know, women fall for that type.' She leaned over and patted Jamie's arm. 'Give in, dearie. Let's face it, you haven't got a chance against him.'

Velma left after a few minutes of shop gossip, and for a while Jamie sat in her chair, the economics book open on her lap. She warned herself not to be too thrilled about Tom's note, but she refused to listen. She tried to concentrate on the economist's opinions of the swing in the attitude of the world market, but her eyes kept straying to the note from Tom. Finally she had to admit that the world market could buy itself out for all she cared at that moment. The book went skittering across the floor as she jumped up and hurried to the bedroom.

What was she going to wear to have dinner on a steamboat? She searched her closet, looking at every dress as if they had sneaked on to the hangers when her back was turned. She started to worry about the quality of her dressier clothing. She had provided herself with inexpensive work outfits that were in keeping with the income of a warehouse clerk, but her dresses were usually bought in New York or San Francisco, and many carried Paris labels. Moreover, in design they looked Parisian. If Tom Malcomb knew his business, he would recognise the quality right away.

But what did it matter? She had made up her mind to tell him the truth, so before the evening was out, he would understand—at least he'd know. She hoped he would understand.

For a moment she stood, pulling at one wayward strand of hair as she worried about his reaction, but then her spirits rose. This was the perfect opportunity to tell him. He was making an apology of sorts. He should be amenable to hers, if she explained it properly.

Since her teenage years, Jamie had been well trained in dressing for the occasion. For years she had chosen her clothes with cool confidence in her taste and donned them with care but no undue concern. But this was the first time she was actually going out with Tom Malcomb on a prearranged date. All her faith in her judgment seemed to leave her as she chose a white silk, a blue linen, a green suit in light wool and several other outfits. She had clothing spread all over her bed by the time she reverted to her original choice and put away everything but the white silk with the nautical collar. The fitted bodice and pleated skirt showed off her slight but rounded figure without being blatant, and the collar was perfect for getting into the spirit of the occasion. The matching jacket would keep away the chill of the late evening.

The agonising choice made, she sat at her dressing table and eyed the reflection in the mirror. She piled her hair on top of her head in a casual, careless effect only a precise arrangement could accomplish.

Satisfied with the effect, she began on her make-up and turned her mind to how she was going to tell Tom Malcomb the truth.

'They say, "a rose by any other name" you know—' That would never do, she thought as she applied a light coating of mascara to her lashes. She'd just have to think of something else. If she went straight into the truth without prefacing it with an explanation, she might not get to explain at all.

'Once upon a time there was a fair damsel who was ruled by a wicked uncle . . .' Would he buy that? She doubted it.

'Well, don't just sit there,' she told her reflection. 'You were so smart two hours ago, come up with something brilliant.'

Her reflection was unco-operative, and when the doorbell rang at seven-thirty, she was still without a plan for telling Tom her true identity.

As she opened the door, the look on his face dispelled any lingering doubts she might have had about her appearance. His was without a fault. The good looks that showed to advantage even in the jeans and sports shirts he wore in the warehouse were enhanced and made elegant by a tailored grey suit worn with the negligence of a man used to the best.

The short drive to the restaurant was filled with desultory conversation, most of it shop talk. Jamie relaxed in the seat of the car and admired his handling of the Jaguar. He drove as if the powerful car was an extension of his personality. She was conscious of his hand near her leg as he shifted the gears smoothly and precisely.

Apparently the name Malcomb had rated some special attention, because they had just crossed the gangway when the door was opened for them and they were shown to a table by the window, overlooking the canal and a grass verge that separated it from the river. The white linen on the tables was perfect for setting off the small brass lanterns and made an excellent backdrop for the teak window frames and furniture. None of the charm of the old boat had been hidden when it had been put to a use the builders could not have visualised.

The menu offered a tempting choice of seafood, and Tom ordered a delicacy for that part of the country, fresh abalone, flown in from the West Coast. They had just been served an impressive crabmeat salad when Tom brought the conversation around to the suggested menu of crow. As usual he was offhand.

'A canal can be considered a back street of a river, can't it?' he said, taking a sip of his white wine.

'The alley off the main street,' Jamie retorted with a

smile to remove any doubts that she was still angry.

'Sometimes they're handy for getting from one place to another,' Tom answered as he started on his salad. 'Not that they're a way of life.'

Jamie kept her eyes down and used the prongs of her salad fork to trace the ruffles on a leaf of romaine lettuce. He had given her the opening she needed to tell him the truth.

'At times they're necessary—when a person has a reason for not coming out in the open. But sooner or later they have to face the lights on the main street—'

'Well, be glad you didn't have to face the main street this evening,' said Tom as he reached for a bread-stick. 'Fridays are always bad, but today was worse than usual. Look at the moon coming up. Guard yourself. Moon in the sky and on the water—double danger.'

Jamie gazed out the window and wondered what had happened. She had had the conversation moving in the right direction, and his interruption had nullified a perfect opportunity. She turned her gaze to Tom as his eyes came up from his salad to meet hers. Those light grey eyes within their dark fringe of lashes were unreadable in the unsteady light of the small brass lantern.

After a perfect dinner they lingered for a while, chatting about commonplaces and absorbing the view. When they left the restaurant, Tom suggested a walk along the path by the canal, and Jamie readily agreed. She was not anxious to have the evening end. Tom was a thoughtful and charming escort, and the nagging guilt of not being honest with him was getting stronger.

Some years before, the city had created a park out of the low land by the river, and picturesque footbridges spanned the canal, giving access to the river bank. Other couples were strolling along in the soft evening air. They appeared in the pools of illumination cast by the evenly spaced gas lamps, and disappeared again in the darkness.

Jamie and Tom walked in a cocoon of isolation, conversing amiably, moving from one subject to another. His arm encircled her waist and she felt the movement of his hip and side as they moved slowly along. Occasionally she could feel his eyes on her, and a pleasant warmth, brought about by his attention, kept her from noticing the cooling evening. Several times she thought she had an opening to bring up the subject foremost on her mind; but each time, before she realised it, the opportunity slipped away. She wondered at the quicksilver changes of subject.

They were on their way back to the car when a breeze brought home to her that she was chilled. She shivered and Tom looked down at her with concern.

'I'm an idiot, keeping you out here,' he said. 'It's a little too early in the year for evening walks.'

'I'll be fine if I have a cup of coffee,' she answered. A plan was forming.

'We'll get you some right away.' Tom looked towards the restaurant again, but she forestalled his suggestion.

'Let's go to my place and I'll make a pot.'

'Oh, have I been promoted to the ranks of the invited?' he teased.

'Of course,' she returned. 'I live on a back street, you know.'

Her true reason was more serious. There was a certain psychological advantage to being on one's own ground. In her own home, she could more easily control the conversation, she thought. At least she could hardly have less ability to maintain a subject long enough to lead it around to making her point.

Back in her apartment, she went immediately to the kitchen and started the coffee while Tom turned on the lights in the living-room.

While she put cups and saucers on a tray, she paused to tick off subjects she might use to get her into her explanation. By the time the coffee maker had ceased to gurgle and gave its final expiring glurp, she was sure of her plan. The china cups would be her opening. What more reasonable subject with which to begin a conversation than to talk about a cup she was filling with coffee?

In the living-room Tom rose and took the tray from her, putting it on the table.

'You know,' he remarked, 'I just looked at your view again. That low building across the way, and the two taller ones on either side, gives you a nice framing for the skyline in the distance.'

As he continued to talk about the view, Jamie poured the coffee, shaking her head slightly at the china cups. How had he done that to her? There were only so many ways she could lead up to her confession. Was he going to thwart them all? At this rate she would remain Jamie Stevens until she was ninety and had forgotten she ever had another name.

'Why so quiet?' asked Tom as he came over to sit by her on the sofa. He took his cup as she offered it, watching her over the rim as he sipped it. Could she use that as an opening? She was desperate enough to try anything.

'I was thinking about people, about how little we know about them,' she said solemnly. 'Think of it—what do you really know about me—' She was interrupted as he put the cup down and leaned over, placing a kiss on her forehead.

'You're a beautiful accomplice,' he said. 'And we're quite a team—the Bonnie and Clyde of hats!'

'No, be serious.' Jamie pulled away slightly, wanting his kiss, his attention, but as Jamie Stone, not as Jamie Stevens. 'You don't know anything about me—'

'Then be the mystery woman in my life, fill it with

romance and intrigue,' he said, catching her up in an embrace and kissing her.

His arms around her, his lips on hers, brought to the surface an entirely different emotion from those she had been suffering. Her desire to tell him her dark secret was lost under a growing fire within her as his lips explored hers. His tongue brought to the surface the tingling excitement on the tender places of her lips, her mouth, and her cheek. As his mouth travelled down her throat to the hollow of her neck, she whimpered with the rising passion within her.

He raised his head, looking into her eyes, his own dark with desire. His hands that had simply held her moved ever so slowly at the small of her back, and the back of her neck, bringing to life sensations that raged like fire up and down her spine. His parted lips emitted no sound as he breathed, but a slight trembling shook them as he slid one hand around her waist and down her hip, creating a sensual awareness in the flesh of her thigh.

Jamie moaned and raised her head, seeking his lips, but instead of meeting her halfway, he held back, still keeping his eyes on hers.

'Kiss me,' she murmured, but with a small shake of his head, he refused.

'I want to look at you,' he whispered, his voice hoarse and out of control. 'I want to see your eyes. Want me, show me you want me—show me with your eyes.' His own expression was half exultant, half hungry. A sensuality played around his lips.

Jamie slid one arm around his back, up his chest, and caressed his throat as her fingers sought to trace the outline of his lips. He gave a small, shuddering sigh, and finding in that sound the power of her ability to give him pleasure, to raise his passions as he raised hers, Jamie ran her fingers through his hair, down his back, bringing out in him the same trembling desire that was consuming her past thought and reason.

While one hand caressed her skin, leaving ripples of fire where his fingers touched, with the other he impatiently threw the pillows on the back of the sofa to the floor. Then gently, as if she were some fragile, precious thing, he slipped one arm around her shoulders, and another under her knees, laying her down on the wide cushions.

She raised her arms, mutely begging him to join her, to lie beside her, to give her the feeling of his strong body next to hers, but again he denied her. Instead he sat, alternately watching her face and his hands as they roamed her body. Through the silk of her dress and the clothing beneath it she felt the warmth of his hands, the fire of his desire as he watched the revealing shape of her breasts, her waist and hips where his hands pressed down her clothing.

Desire for him was raging through her, and she resented the clothing that kept his hands from her skin. Her own fingers were clutching at him, more demanding than loving as he held himself away from her while he built a need in her that threatened to consume her. She twisted with the fire that burned in her, moaning in an exquisite desire that filled her with exultant passion and a pain of longing.

With trembling fingers she pushed at the jacket of his suit, sliding it back over his shoulders until by relaxing his arms he let it fall to the floor. Her hands, tantalising the skin beneath his silk shirt, moved over the pectoral muscles and teased the flesh on his sides until he shuddered and leaned forward.

He stretched his length beside her on the couch. Braced on one elbow, he looked down at her as his right hand stroked her hair, his fingers winding and reshaping the curls.

When his head bent over hers, his kisses were all she desired, passionate, hungry, demanding. Jamie gave back in full measure and added her own needs. For long moments they were locked together in a passionate embrace, drawing back to savour the delight before their lips touched again.

With nothing in her mind but her enjoyment of his expression of love, Jamie allowed herself to soar with her passions. She felt lifted, rarefied, ten miles above the earth, but knowing she didn't travel alone. She could feel in Tom the same mood, see the joy and pleasure in his eyes.

Her arms were around him, holding him close, listening to his heartbeat, watching the rapid beat of his pulse in his throat when he drew back for a moment. Gradually she realised their kisses were less passionate, less demanding. The fury of their desire had somehow passed. The passing, she knew, had begun in him and not in herself.

She held him, wondering what had happened. They had been so fiery in their need, and her flesh resented the lost opportunity. But her mind, the interpreter of her vision, recognised the emotional giving and taking in his eyes, recognised a regret in the tenderness with which he was bringing their moment of passion to an end.

Her flesh wanted her to cry out that now was no time to stop. Her heart told her he regretted holding back more than she.

'Why?' Jamie's question was full of sympathy for his regret, even if she needed a reason for his withdrawal.

Tom's smile was slow, tender and partially forced. 'Maybe it's because you don't live on Main Street.' No answer, an attempt to carry on a joke that no longer had meaning, but she refused to push.

What right had she to demand honesty of him, when she gave him none? Did he feel that? As they sat up on the couch, Jamie straightened her hair while Tom busied himself picking up his discarded jacket and replacing the cushions on the back of the sofa. She wondered if the discrepancy between her clothing, the furnishings, and the job she held was too wide a gap for him to accept. As she picked up the cup of now cold coffee and held it primly in her hands, her eyes turned to him. The question must have showed.

He opened his mouth, closed it and swallowed before he tried again. The cool poise was for a moment diminished.

'When something is important—really important, you don't just grab what you want and run.'

Suddenly Jamie was shaken. Her feelings for him had been so sudden and intense she had not stopped to really think about his. How could she feel herself in love with someone and not give him credit for sensitivity and a sense of values? How could she be so blind when everything around him had pointed to it? His office in the main store had showed careful thought, his deliberate efforts to remain blind to the silly games in the warehouse during a slack period, showed his deep understanding of the needs of people. Surely he could not be any different in love?

What would have been her feelings later if he had not drawn back from their lovemaking? She had been tortured several times by wondering why he was bothering with a clerk, if his reason for seeing her had been some casual flirtation, something he would not want others to know about. She raised her eyes to meet his again. That was what he said. What she took to be a play on their running joke had carried a serious meaning.

Suddenly she leaned over and kissed him on the cheek, lightly, but with all the gratitude in her soul.

'Was that for something special?' His smile was soft.

'For something very special.' Jamie's voice sang with

happiness. 'One day, a long time from now, I'll tell you about it.'

'It will have to be another day,' said Tom. 'I'd better get out of here before I wear out my welcome.'

You'll never do that, Jamie wanted to tell him as he slipped on his jacket. She walked him to the door. He put one hand on the knob and hesitated. Then he turned and took her in his arms, giving her a long, tender kiss.

After a blissful moment, Jamie pulled back and smiled up at him. 'It was a beautiful evening, Mr Malcomb.'

His smile was lazy, content. 'I agree, Miss Stevens.'

The name was a knife, leaving a slash of guilt across her consciousness. She knew she could not let him walk through that door without telling him the truth.

'My name is Stone,' she blurted out, drawing in a breath in reaction to her own stupidity. How could she have been such an idiot? Without any explanation, what could he think but that she had deliberately set out to make a fool of him? What her reasoning would have been, she was not clear, but without any prelude, he was left to think the worst.

She waited, fearing his reaction. So far there had been none. His hands, still on her waist, had not moved by a fingertip. His eyes even retained that slightly surprised and puzzled expression, as if he had missed the meaning of what she said. Hardly daring to breathe, she was driven to desperation by the suspense.

'Well, *say* something,' she pleaded, a slight tremble in her voice.

'I'm not sure of my lines,' Tom said quietly. 'Do I rage and tear my hair—play the understanding big brother, or stalk out into the night, never again to be seen by mortal man?' A smile was curling his lips.

Jamie stared at him in incredulity, not believing the calm humour she was watching. 'You mean that's *it*? I've been driving myself crazy wondering how to tell you and you're not angry or—or anything?'

'It's that anything I'm having trouble with,' he said quietly. 'Call my part guilt. I knew what you were doing. I've been trying to stop you all evening.' His eyes had turned serious now. 'You see, I knew all along. I knew you'd given your word to George—' he hesitated, and Jamie felt the importance he put on those last words, though he had not emphasised them in any way. 'I'm glad it's out in the open, though. I'm not much good at duplicity either. The night I had dinner here, I almost gave it away by mentioning George.'

As he pulled her close again, Jamie leaned against him, weakened with relief that a dread had come to nothing. For the moment she gave no thought to the additional evidence that George had broken his word. Tom was not angry, he would not stalk out into the night, leaving her miserable with the knowledge that she had destroyed their relationship. For some minutes they were still, just enjoying their first honest closeness. Then Jamie thought of what he had said about giving away the secret.

'You mentioned my uncle that night,' she said.

'Um-hum—I thought you'd catch that right away,' he said.

'I did, but I was so nervous, I thought I'd slipped up—I hate being dishonest—and while we're on that subject, I didn't just give my word to Uncle George. We had a bargain—an "I do if you do" type thing, and he broke it. He wasn't to tell anyone who I was, and neither would I. He told you.'

'No,' said Tom, laughter in his denial. 'Actually, he told Dad, I got it second hand.'

'Either way, he broke his word, so I'm no longer obligated to live a lie.' She pulled away slightly to look him in the eye. 'And my job on the platform became available because they transferred Cleo Knowles very suddenly. Now I don't believe I ended up on the receiving platform by accident.'

'Of course not.' Tom's face was suddenly unreadable. 'But now that the choice is yours, will you stay—or go into the store?'

'I'll stay.' Jamie moved back a step to better judge his reactions. 'I guess Uncle George wanted me to see some of the rougher side of the business, and I've learned a lot—' she paused, seeing the twitch of his lips. She must sound like a know-it-all after only two weeks on the job. 'I know there's much more to learn—' She could tell by his expression she had misjudged what he had been thinking. The disbelief that flickered in those beautiful grey eyes was suddenly covered. Covered by a bland, patronising expression.

'I'm wrong in my assessment,' she stated the fact she read in his eyes. Her mind was searching for alternatives.

'Oh, no, you'll learn a lot,' he replied, the falsity of his tone telling her he was staying with a safer subject rather than step into a dangerous truth.

'Wait a minute,' Jamie demanded, her eyes narrowing. 'You *know* why I was put on that platform! Tell me.'

Tom hesitated. For the first time he seemed genuinely unsure of himself. 'It's an embarrassing question for *me* to have to answer.'

The truth hit Jamie like a hammer. Now, all those questions George Stone had asked about Tom fixing her car and having dinner in her apartment took on meaning. His interest in who she saw during the day, what she thought of the Malcomb's administration as well as theirs, took on another meaning. What she had thought was a competitive spirit was a sly game of a different sort.

'You mean he's matchmaking—you and me—? That old devil!'

Tom nodded, his eyes laughing. 'Both of them. My dad's in it with him. And it's time you recognised them for what they are.'

She stood quite still, letting these new ideas sort themselves out. But as various implications took form, one fact stood out head and shoulders above the manipulations of the two older men. Tom had known what they had in mind and had allowed himself to be used. She respected him for listening to his father—only a fool ignored the benefit of experience—but if he had allowed his parent to dictate, even in matters of the heart, then Tom Malcomb was not the man she thought him.

'You knew and you went along with it?' she accused, not believing it could be true, but seeing no other answer.

'Now wait a minute,' he said sharply, his eyes blazing with sudden anger as he caught her meaning. 'I wasn't all that sure at first—not until Dad developed a sudden interest in the S. & S. employees. I'll admit I suspected, though. And just to make sure they didn't succeed, I came on that platform the first day you were there, determined to be the biggest bastard in two hemispheres.'

Jamie remembered their initial argument and smiled. 'I thought you were.'

'I planned it,' Tom smiled too, his flash of anger lost under the memory. 'But there you were, looking fourteen and lost, scattering diamonds all over the floor, and I couldn't keep it up. But I tried again, you know. I left on a nasty note.' His look said he deserved some credit for that.

'It's a wonder you didn't ignore me entirely.'

'I tried to. I can hold my own against Dad and George, but you kept bowling me over.' To prove it, he gave her a kiss on the cheek.

Jamie returned the kiss and then stepped away again.

The relief his understanding had brought was being lost under her outrage that she had been used in a plot.

'The next time I come rolling down the alley, you'll have to keep your feet,' she said sharply. She paced across the small living-room and came back to shake one slender finger at him. 'They can't be allowed to get away with it. If we let them manage our lives now, they'll never quit. We'll end up as nothing but store models.'

As Tom heard her out, he leaned back against the door, his hands in his pockets, his eyes darkening with worry.

'In principle I agree, but have you thought of the alternative? Do we stop seeing each other because they decided we should get together?' He shook his head. 'You're in my life now, and too important to risk. I'd rather fight it out over something else.'

Jamie threw herself into his arms, seeking shelter from her conflicting emotions. She loved him for his honesty, and to even think of never seeing him again was painful. But all her life she had been drilled for a responsibility, and if she wanted to turn her back on it, she had no idea how to do so. To be in his arms was to be safe, protected, to take his assessment of the situation would prevent any painful decisions on her part, but her training had been too thorough. She pulled away, turning her back on him. Her voice was quiet when she spoke—not quite steady, but she could hear her own resolution.

'I love you, Tom, but I still can't let them get away with it. Our positions are not the same. You've been with Malcomb's long enough to assert your authority, to prove you're your own person. I've just arrived—I was bullied into the warehouse, and tricked—' she let the words hang. How could she say that even though she had been given exactly what she wanted, it was important that the decision be hers, not her uncle's? But the necessity of saying it was taken from her. She felt Tom's hands on her shoulders, not a romantic touch, but one full of support and understanding.

'You want the right to make your own decisions,' his voice was strong, carrying a tinge of worry so evident in his face that she had turned away from it. 'But where will that leave us?'

'I don't *know!*' she wailed, turning again to hide in his embrace. 'Why do things have to be in such a tangle?'

He held her close for a moment. 'We'll work it out,' he murmured into her hair. 'We'll end up in another mess, and they'll win this one, you know. It's hard to fight a war when we're all on the same side.' This time he pushed her away. With one finger he brushed away a tear on her cheek. 'But if it's that important to you, we'll make them fight for their victory. Now go and put on another pot of coffee. We've got some planning to do!'

CHAPTER EIGHT

VELMA stirred her coffee with a vengeance. 'When you're the big cheese up in the offices, you may fire me for it, sweetie, but I'll tell you right now, you were a fool.'

One of the butterfly pins in her blonde hair threatened to fall out as she jerked her head up to meet Jamie's gaze.

They were taking their midmorning break in the cafeteria at Jamie's suggestion. She wanted Velma's advice, though she wasn't finding it palatable.

'Then I'd be twice a fool, wouldn't I?' Jamie retorted. She was irritated at Velma's reaction, partly because she was having second thoughts herself. The plans she had so blithely made with Tom the night before appeared stupid in the light of day. He had tried to tell her so, but gave way to her insistence. Now she was wishing she had listened, but what could she do? She tried again to explain it, wanting to find that spark of brilliance she had felt in the middle of the night.

'This Daphne is an old friend of his, and he said himself he wouldn't agree if Daphne wasn't in town. He's known her for ages—since they were kids. He's going to tell her the truth—all about us and what we're doing. She's just come out of a bad marriage, and is at a loose end. She'll probably enjoy getting out, taking part in what he calls our next "scrape".'

Velma still looked unconvinced.

'Honey, let me tell you something. I've had enough husbands to know. When a marrying woman comes out of one marriage, she's usually looking for another man to build up her ego. And if the man she finds does the job, she holds on to him.'

'Velma, don't *tell* me things like that!' Jamie stared at the wall, frowning. 'Don't you see—I was so determined to prove to Uncle George that I could handle my own life—'

'That you're cutting off your nose to spite your face, as the old saying goes,' the older woman retorted.

'I was so positive everything would work out,' Jamie muttered. 'The whole idea looked great last night. I was so sure I could come up with someone to parade in front of Uncle George, and now I wonder, where am I going to find a man?' Her voice had been rising without her realising it, and when two Malcomb's warehouse workers turned, interest in their eyes, Jamie wanted to sink under the table.

'With announcements like that, you'll get one!' hissed Velma.

Jamie refused to answer the obvious. She leaned forward, keeping her voice down.

'The only thing to do is to tell him the truth—that in the light of day, I think the whole idea was stupid.'

'Believe me, dearie,' Velma smiled, and patted her hand, 'a man never minds a woman being stupid as long as she lets him be smart. My fifth husband, Harry—no, he was the fourth—anyway, you're doing the right thing.'

'It was just because I was so *mad* at Uncle George,' Jamie explained again. But why explain all that again? The important thing was to get to Tom and let him know their famous plan was off. He was right, they could assert independence another way. Tom had no need to prove himself. She could find another means of letting George Stone know she was her own person with her own mind. With Tom adding his moral support, she'd have no trouble at all. She could do it alone, but somehow, to think of doing anything without Tom's presence and approval was uncomfortable.

When she returned to the warehouse platform she started for the door that led into Malcomb's, and met Hugh Belmont as he was returning.

'I need to see Tom Malcomb for a moment,' she said in explanation, hoping he would not ask why.

'He's not there today,' Hugh replied.

Jamie stared at him, not believing Tom would not be available when she needed to talk to him so desperately.

'Where is he? When will he be back?' she demanded.

Hugh shrugged. 'Monday, I guess. Some big meeting, planning another branch, from what I could get out of his secretary. Probably that new shopping centre up north—we're already signed up for it, I hear. At least I hope it's that. If they have another branch, we'll have one.' He looked around to make sure no one was close enough to overhear. 'And I warn you, Miss Stone— more stores mean more merchandise—if this platform gets much busier, we can't keep up. We'll lose half the stuff we take in.'

For a moment Jamie ceased to be a warehouse clerk and became the executive of her training. She patted him on the shoulder.

'We'll work it out, Hugh. Let me get a little more familiar with the building and we'll do some planning of our own.' Actually she had told him nothing and made no promises, but he was nodding with a renewed confidence. He walked off, probably already searching his mind for answers. By the time she was free to explore the problem with him, he would have the solution mapped out.

At the moment she had no time to worry about the running of the warehouse. Her own life and problems were taking all her energy. She grabbed the clipboard and went out to log in the shipments that had piled up on the dock while she and Velma had been at coffee break. Carl and Freddy were busy running the belt, still clearing away a large, varied delivery that had clogged most of the open space.

Jamie wrote automatically as she considered what she should do. She would not be able to see Tom until Monday. Their plan was for both of them to have dates for the evening. When Tom walked into the country club with Daphne, and Jamie with her date, the two old matchmakers should be thrown into a frenzy. Tom would have Daphne for company. She had been so sure the night before that she could have a date if she chose to. Now where was she to find one?

In the heat of her plan, she had forgotten she was a stranger in town. Why hadn't Tom reminded her of that? Was that why he had smiled so suddenly? He probably thought she would be unable to get a date on the spur of the moment. She jumped to her conclusion and landed flat-footed. New in town or no, her ego was at stake.

'I've *got* to have a man!' she announced with decision.

The sudden quiet from the direction of the belt caused her to cringe. She looked up to see both Carl and Freddy staring at her. Freddy looked disbelieving; Carl smiled hopefully. Jamie's glare sent them back to work with renewed speed.

They were both too young, and her uncle might recognise them; he was proud of his memory for faces and names. She wondered for a moment about Hugh. That would really give Uncle George cause for wonder—a man within the company with eyes for the boss. No, Hugh was in her uncle's confidence, and she had to be able to trust her escort. Nothing would make her use another person as she had been used—both she and Tom had agreed on that. Then she remembered seeing a picture in his office of a pretty woman and two children.

She looked again at Carl and Freddy as they were busy

running the belt. Carl looked older than his eighteen years, but if her uncle checked, he would learn the truth. Besides, how would she separate them? They were so close one never seemed to go anywhere without each other. Two men would not do.

The afternoon wore on and her frustration grew. At three she went into Tom's office in the Malcomb's warehouse and left a message for him. The secretary had been surprised, and Jamie fobbed her off, trying to create an impression of importance and urgency without alarming the girl.

She was back on the platform, ready to close up for the day, when a lone truck backed into the bay.

Oh, no! Jamie thought as she raced out on the platform, recognising the truck. Getting out was the bearded giant of Wednesday night. The last thing she needed was another large load to keep her tied up on the platform with Carl and Freddy gone. This fellow was going to learn to come in on time!

When the big amiable character came around the side of the vehicle, Jamie was already shaking her head. The ends of his heavy moustache fell as his smile faded.

'I'm sure sorry, but this old crate breaks down every time I turn around, otherwise I'd be here on time.'

Today he was without the decorated leather jacket. She noticed the name Mac had been inexpertly embroidered on his denim shirt.

'The platform will be open at seven Monday morning,' she replied sharply. 'And don't tell me you'll be in trouble with your terminal manager. If they can't give you a better truck they can't expect you to be on time.'

He studied the concrete at his feet. When his eyes met hers again, his expression was guarded, as if he expected some blow, but would not flinch. 'But it's not their truck. It's mine—I haul on contract. Another two months and I'll have the money for a down-payment on a better one.

I'm starting my own business, you see.'

Jamie paused. He was getting to her again. With her own problems she had no time to handle his shipment, but she was having trouble facing his disappointment. As if he realised that, he added what he could as a palliative.

'I'll be glad to load the stuff on the belt for you. I know I'm asking a lot—but you see, if I have to come back here Monday morning, then I'll miss getting my pick-ups for the day. I'll be out a day's work.'

Jamie paused, temporarily disconcerted. She had never depended on a day's pay because of her large income. Since she had no idea what hardship the loss of one could bring, she was afraid to lay that penalty on someone else. With a sigh, she capitulated.

'Oh, okay—but you owe me,' she warned him as she started back to the office for her clipboard.

'Anything I can do,' he called after her.

Anything he could do . . . The thought crept around in her head on tiny feet as she listed his cargo.

Again he had brought another large shipment, but within the confines of the truck he sorted it out into departments before putting it on the belt to her instruction. Jamie sent each order around on the belt system. In the past two days she had learned to operate the semi-automatic machinery properly. In twenty minutes the platform was clear again.

During that time the big bearded driver repeated his depth of gratitude with every carton he put on the belt. Jamie had been busy thinking, and when the last load had gone around the corner, she turned to look him over critically.

'I really am grateful,' he said again. 'If you ever need help—'

'I need help,' Jamie said abruptly. 'And you owe me a favour.'

'Anything,' he said.

'I need a temporary boy-friend.' She rushed to push out the words before she lost her nerve. The words were no sooner out than she wished them back. The bearded giant paled; if he had been asked to escort the Medusa, he could not have looked more unwilling! That was a blow Jamie's ego didn't need. Unconsciously her hand went to her hair. She wondered if her face was smudged with dirt. The dress code of practicality for the warehouse forbade silks and satins, but surely her appearance wouldn't send a man into a panic.

'But—but lady, I'm engaged, and my girl would never let me get away with that!'

She was surprised that the obvious answer had eluded her reasoning. Behind that bristling beard was a good-looking man, and judging by her short conversation with him, he was an honourable, hardworking man. Certainly some woman would have recognised that. Still, disappointment was her predominant thought.

'I guess you have big plans for the weekend too,' she said. With her own romance in a mess, she could only wish happiness to others whose love life was running smoothly. No one's need justified bringing them problems. She would just have to look elsewhere.

'No, she's out of town for two weeks, but—'

'Oh?' Jamie's eyes came up to his. Maybe the situation was more hopeful than she thought. 'If she's not around, then she wouldn't know if you were at home waiting patiently or not.'

He shuffled his feet, clearly uncomfortable in saying no, but adamant. 'Susie expects it,' he spoke slowly, as if he were going to be the butt of a joke for his attitude, but ready to take her scorn. 'I have to think of her and what's good for us.'

Jamie's eyes narrowed. She disliked herself in advance for what she was going to do, but she was desperate. Her Stone blood came to the top as she made up her mind to drive a hard bargain.

'Then maybe you'd better think of her. How long before you can buy another truck?'

He looked up warily. 'A couple of months with good luck, but what does that have to do—'

'Suppose this old rig keeps breaking down—what if you can't deliver late shipments here any more—or suppose you could count on being able to deliver here as along as I was on the platform—'

Jamie let the words hang, not realising at the moment that she was leaving them like a threat over his head. She was sick with what she had done; she was using the power of her position for coercion. She was ready to retract her threat when she saw she had won.

'But, lady, if she ever found out—'

Jamie struggled with her conscience. Blackmail was a nasty word, but she decided she deserved it. Still, there was some justification. Suppose this huge hunk of a man got lonely while his Susie was out of town? Susie should thank her. Jamie would keep him busy for a while, and he was certainly safe with her.

'We'll arrange it so she doesn't,' she said decisively. She had her man and she wasn't going to let him get away. He was perfect for what she needed. If he was that interested in his girl, there was no possibility he would be hurt by the game she and Tom were playing. A truck driver, saving money to buy other vehicles, would not circulate at the Country Club, where she was to have dinner with her uncle. His girl would never have to know.

'Come with me,' she ordered, and led him into her small office and closed the door. First she swore him to secrecy, then she told him the truth behind her being on the platform. Halfway through the story he developed some interest, but when she told him they would be going to the Fair Oaks Country Club that night, he almost backed out.

'I don't know,' he said uneasily, reaching for the door knob. 'If Mr Stone didn't like it, he could keep me from delivering here—or maybe Mr Malcomb would bar me from his store.'

'Don't be foolish!' Jamie snapped. She might be angry with George Stone, but she was certain he would never stoop to taking out his anger on an innocent person. Since she wouldn't admit her knowledge of George's plans, he would never know of the deliberate attempt to thwart him.

'You just be at this address at seven-thirty, and wear a coat and tie. I understand that's the uniform of the day.' The 'I understand' had been an attempt to soften the instructions. Still looking unconvinced, and for all the world like a five-year-old caught in some mischief, Mac ambled back to his truck and drove off.

Not until she was dressing that night, and gleefully planning how she was going to introduce that gentle grizzly bear to her uncle, did Jamie realise she had never even asked his last name.

'Mac Lumas,' he told her that evening as he drove his battered old Ford away from the door of her apartment house. He was nervous, and looked slightly uncomfortable in the dark suit and tie. But Jamie was pleased to see that while his clothing lacked the tailored elegance of Tom Malcomb's, he would not be sneered at by the other patrons because of his attire. She had suffered pangs of worry while she dressed, wondering if, in her anxiety to fill her part of the bargain with Tom, she would be letting Mac in for embarrassment.

'Now, don't worry,' she said as they walked into the club. 'I hope you dance—I hear an orchestra tuning up.'

'Probably not what they do here,' he answered

morosely as the major-domo came forward.

Fair Oaks, Jamie knew, was 'the' country club of th
area. As the oldest and most exclusive, it stood head an
shoulders above its newer, more fashionably locate
contemporaries. It drew the local cream of membershi
who took their ease in a well worn elegance none of th
up-and-coming clubs could afford. They were led to th
dining room where pale blue damask upholstery an
creamy French provincial furniture added warmth an
charm to the pale blue tablecloths with their precis
settings of china, silver and crystal.

At a table near the far corner of the room she sav
George Stone, looking thunderous. At the adjoinin
table, looking equally out of humour, was the man wit
the white leonine hair, Tom, and one of the mos
beautiful brunettes Jamie had ever seen. She would hav
been intimidated by the beauty of the woman if she ha
not seen the look on Tom's face. Jamie knew he woul
recognise Mac, and had half dreaded a smirk, since h
would probably know she had somehow coerced the bi
truck driver. Tom's expression was speculative
apparently he too respected the big man as she ha
learned to do earlier in the day.

Jamie could not have been happier with the look o
her uncle's face, and as she recognised the man with th
white hair to be Tom's father, his expression made he
happy too. Only the beauty of the woman to whom To
was paying an unwonted amount of attention alloyed he
joy.

When they approached the table, the look on Georg
Stone's face was worth all the worry and frustration o
the day. His jaw dropped, his drink tipped, a few drop
of amber liquid fell on the tablecloth. When he rose t
greet his niece, Jamie thought he looked a little u
steady.

'Hello, Uncle.' She stepped forward and gave him

kiss on the cheek. She introduced Mac, giving no details, thinking if it were a legitimate date she would probably have left the men to discover for themselves their common interests. Would she? What was natural? Suddenly she couldn't seem to remember what it was like to behave like an ordinary person, with only one name and no secrets.

Her gaze lifted over the table arrangements to see how her date was affecting Tom, but if he noticed at all he was cool about it. He was leaning over to hear what the brunette was saying. Well, two could play at that game, thought Jamie, raging inside. She focused her attention on the questions her uncle was asking Mac. Remembering the look on George's face when they entered the dining room, she felt it her duty to protect her hulking bear from her uncle's displeasure, but for some reason, that was rapidly disappearing.

'Just local deliveries, huh?' George asked Mac.

'That's all right now,' Mac answered each question with more ease, since they were on a subject obviously close to his heart. 'You have to start somewhere, and I can't take that old heap out on long hauls.'

George Stone had bragged to his niece that he still knew every facet of the multi-million-dollar business they headed, and as he discussed short-hauling with Mac, Jamie could believe it. She watched that gleam in his eye and wondered if he was really enjoying himself as much as he appeared to be.

She was being left out of the conversation, and from her position at the table, the view straight ahead of her was Tom, complete with the brunette at his side. Since he gave every evidence of being totally captivated by the conversation at his own table, she could have been back in Arizona for all the attention he paid her. She was growing increasingly unhappy with the evening when George turned to the elder Malcomb and suggested he would be interested in their talk.

'In fact, why are we at separate tables?' he asked suddenly—too suddenly. 'We're all friends here. Let's see if we can get a better arrangement.'

The 'better arrangement' was a larger table near the middle of the room. Jamie's quick eye caught the whisking away of the Reserved sign immediately after George had raised his hand to the head waiter. The move was too smoothly made, dinner arrived too soon after they were seated at the new table for the complication to have occurred without advance planning.

Very clever, Jamie thought. Very clever too were the new seating arrangements. Mac was to her right, her uncle and then Abel were to her left. George was throwing questions at her escort until he was left no time to even speak to her. Across the table she was again in full view of Tom as he gave his attention to Daphne. This was manipulation, she decided.

Only once during dinner did Tom's eyes meet hers, giving her reassurance, but most of the time she was condemned by the conversation to eat her meal in silence. The chef at Fair Oaks was well known, but she could have been eating straw for all she noticed. Her mind was occupied trying to find a way out of her uncomfortable position.

By the time the plates had been removed, the band was playing. When Tom led Daphne on to the dance floor, Mac was reminded of his duties as escort and asked Jamie to dance. He was a good dancer, and she would have enjoyed whirling in his arms to the music, but every time they turned, she could see Tom and Daphne as the girl in the white dress looked up at those light grey eyes and smiled. Don't hate her, it was your idea, Jamie told herself. A lot that mattered, she thought.

*   *   *

Back at the table, Abel glared into his drink.

'Stop glowering,' said George as soon as the dancers were out of earshot.

'What went wrong with the plan?' Abel demanded.

'Nothing.' George leaned back in his chair and watched the dancers. His face showed his satisfaction. 'They're working together better than even we thought they would.'

Abel drained his glass and signalled for another. 'For them to start seeing other people wasn't what *I* had in mind.'

'Don't be stampeded,' George grinned. 'If one of them had shown up with a date we could worry. But both of them? Somehow they figured out what we had in mind and they're fighting us.' He raised his brows, his look turned sly. 'But they're fighting us *together*. Stop worrying, sit back and enjoy. Don't let them be the ones to leave laughing.'

Jamie was glad when the evening was over. The only light of the evening was her one dance with Tom, and that was a fast number. He could have made a better choice, she thought, but she knew circumstances had not given him much leeway.

When Mac took her home she discovered to her dismay that her uncle had invited the two of them to dinner the next night at his home. Mac, professing to her that he had not known what else to do, accepted the invitation.

'Oh, I don't think that was necessary,' Jamie told him. 'I can cancel that.'

Mac appeared to have two expressions, a smile and a slow, stoic look that hid a good brain. No change of expression alerted Jamie to his disappointment, but the big man seemed to shrink slightly.

'You want to go?' she asked, unbelieving. 'I thought

you were so worried about Susie.'

'Susie's a big reason,' Mac said slowly. 'Mr Stone said we'd talk about a contract. That would mean a lot to me, and Susie and I could get married. We want a family, so I don't want her to work.'

'Oh,' said Jamie, sympathising with any romance, and thinking how nice it would be to have children running around the house. But something else bothered her.

'Mac, don't get your hopes too high. I don't think Uncle George would mean to hurt you, but I'm sure he knows what we're up to. He could be stringing you along.'

Mac kept both hands on the wheel and his eyes on the road. His voice was thoughtful. 'I know he was at first. But he got interested because I offered him a good deal. He's a smart man, Miss Stone, and he knows what's up in the business.'

'We'll go,' Jamie sighed. After all, she had brought Mac into the tangle, and if he was able to benefit by it, she should help him, she decided. He might be the only one.

The baby face under the bristling beard looked thoughtful. 'You brought me into this, and if he wants to talk about contracting short-hauls, can you blame me for listening?'

In her apartment, Jamie threw her wrap and purse on the bed and went back to the living-room where there was more room for pacing. Something had gone wrong. George Stone had been upset when they first walked into the club, but later on he was enjoying himself. By the time the evening was over, he was actually encouraging Mac. What was she going to do now? And Tom had looked so—so interested in Daphne.

Velma was right: she was a complete fool. She had come to that irrevocable decision when the doorbell rang. If her uncle had stopped by to gloat she was going to choke him, she decided, and flung the door wide ready to do battle.

She stepped back in fear as she faced the half-turned figure in the trench coat and wide-brimmed felt hat. She felt all the fear conditioned by the movie villains with their hat brims pulled down and their coat collars turned up to hide their faces. Then she realised that was exactly what she was seeing. The head turned and a pair of silvery grey eyes peered at her between the narrow space of the camouflage.

'Agent 409?' whispered Tom.

'Is that you, Mr Clean?' Jamie asked, her heart soaring out of frustration.

He stepped in and she closed the door. He removed the trench coat and hat and took her in his arms. After a long kiss he freed her from his embrace and stood back to look at her.

'You're beautiful tonight, but I know no one appreciated it as I did. I missed you today.'

She wanted to retort, thinking how much she had wanted to see him, and how his keeping his attention on Daphne all evening had not been true evidence of his feelings. But that would be catty, especially when he had been with Daphne at Jamie's own insistence. Had she expected him to be boorish to the other woman? Certainly not.

'I missed you too,' she said. 'And I think our plans were all for nothing. Uncle George's reaction wasn't at all what I expected.'

'Oh, we gave him a few bad moments,' Tom said placidly, then taking her hand, he led her to the couch. When they were seated, and his arm was around her shoulders, for the first time that day she felt real, whole again. For a few minutes they sat quietly, his fingers playing idly on her shoulder, his other hand holding hers.

This was a big part of love, she thought, enjoying the quiet while they rested, letting the outside world and its concerns drift away. The silence, the light touch of their bodies that communicated through their skin, carried messages of reassurance, of support, of togetherness. All the fears of the morning, the need to see Tom to call of their plan, and the misery of watching him with another girl vanished as, sitting by him, she absorbed his nearness. After a while her sigh of contentment seemed to bring him back out of his own thoughts. He smiled down at her.

'This is where I wanted to be,' he said softly. 'I thought the evening would never end.'

'You thought so!' Jamie could not help retorting. 'I was caught between Uncle George and Mac, and I thought, before the evening was over, they were going to call in a lawyer and merge companies!'

Tom's mobile brows snapped down. 'They seemed to be getting along pretty well.'

'I wasn't needed at all,' Jamie muttered, her voice showing she was still a little stung over being left out of the conversation at dinner.

'By me you were,' Tom's mood suddenly lightened and he raised her face to kiss her long and gently.

She surrendered to his embrace, her arms encircling him, holding him close. In his arms, with him in hers, all her hurts healed again and she resolved not to open the wounds again, to let them heal so that nothing interrupted her desire for him, so nothing kept her from feeling the desire, the warmth that flooded from his strong hard body to hers.

His kiss became more urgent and she met it with rising fire. She swirled upward in the spirit of their togetherness, knowing this was what she wanted, this was what her being craved.

Her hands communicated their wants as they kneaded

the strong muscles of his back, his neck and entangled themselves in his hair. Her breath seemed to leave her as all her strength centred itself to fan that growing furnace he had ignited with his touch.

His lips left hers and paused to rest on her cheek. Slightly parted, they allowed his breath to pass through, the heat of it warmed the side of her face. Slowly, with tiny flicks of his tongue, he fed the warmth to fire.

'I love you,' he whispered as his lips moved to touch the lobe of her ear, the smooth sensitive skin beneath the line of her jaw.

Jamie wanted to answer with more than the soft moan that filled her throat, but the words were lost under the weight of her emotions that threatened to burst the bounds of her being, to tear her in pieces, ripping from her all existence but him, his love, the pleasure his hands and lips offered. Instead of words, she tightened her hold, kissed his forehead, his temples, and pulling back because of the need to recapture a part of her spinning emotions, she touched his lips with her fingertips. She loved that mouth that could change from laughter to a sensuality she had never dreamed possible.

As she touched him he stilled, his eyes alight in a passion of exultation. he seemed to be lost to everything but her hands as her fingers played over his jawline, traced the outer shell of his ear and by way of his cheek found his lips again.

His eyes slitted against the light as he remained immovable, as if even a breath would stop her caress. This was the force of love, Jamie thought with wonder. That one person could affect another so profoundly was a power greater than all the world's wealth could create. It was both terrible and wonderful, but to exercise it to the fullest extent, it must be shared.

'I love you,' she forced the words past the restriction in the throat. Just speaking brought an end to the pressure within her. Now she saw clearly what had held her back. Some vague fear of surrendering her heart had been tearing her apart. With that shadowy demon destroyed, what had burst forth was her need to love, to give, to offer the most precious of her possessions, herself. Only by freeing part of herself, could she hope to accept him. 'I love you, I love you, I love you,' she sang in the ecstasy of her emotional release.

'With that between us, we can't lose,' Tom answered. He pulled her close to him, her head against his chest, his chin resting lightly on her head. For some moments she was lost in the awareness of her own feelings before she realised their lovemaking had stopped. As inexplicably as the night before, Tom had let it drift off into a never-never-land of unfulfilled desire. The moment was gone, and with it came another regret, puzzlement, pain.

She drew back and looked at him, her confusion in her eyes, but he sat with his back, gazing up at the ceiling.

'Do I have cobwebs?' she asked, knowing the hurt and frustration was in her voice, but not able to contain it.

'Not that I can see,' he answered, his eyes still on the flat white surface.

'I don't understand,' said Jamie, wanting a better answer than he had given her the night before.

Tom dropped his hand from her shoulder and stood up, walking over to the window, where he moved the curtain with one hand and looked down on the street. She could see the tension in his every movement, in every line of his body, in the hand that gripped the curtain so tightly it would be wrinkled when he freed it.

'It's still a back street,' he said quietly.

Jamie, sighed, wishing for the nth time she had kept her temper when she came out of that broom closet. With a sinking heart she wondered how they could have a relationship of any kind when he never seemed to forget. She had forgiven him his moment of bad temper.

'How long do I have to pay for that remark?' she asked.

He turned, letting the curtain fall. The wrinkles showed. His eyes were dark, his face stiff.

'No longer than I will,' he said shortly.

'Can't you forget I said it—' the pain overrode what she intended to be an apology.

'It doesn't matter whether it was said or not,' Tom said slowly. 'It's the truth, and that's what I can't forget. Why are we going through this foolishness? Why can't we send Daphne off with your truck driver and forget the whole silly game?' One long arm shot out, pointing to the coat and hat on the chair by the door. 'That was a joke when I bought it, but it's not funny any more. And sneaking around corners is not for me—not for my life.'

'I was a fool to even suggest it,' sighed Jamie, rising to join him by the window. She told him about her desire to stop the farce before it had even begun, but his absence from the warehouse had prevented her from seeing him.

'Then we've seen the last of those two,' Tom said as he walked to the door, picking up his coat and hat. His eyes were laughing as he slipped into the trench coat and pulled the hat down over his eyes, thought better of that idea and pushed it back on his head.

After a long good night kiss that set all Jamie's nerves tingling again, he pulled the brim down and opened the door.

'I'll sneak off into the night, a shadow unseen by even the forces of darkness—' His eyes turned serious as he opened the door. 'The architect stayed over, so I have to see him tomorrow morning. But about three I'll pick you up, and there'll be no more nonsense about sneaking around. From now on it's out in the open.'

'I'll be ready,' said Jamie, her smile of delight dying as she remembered the plans made between her uncle and

Mac. How was she going to reach him to let him know he was free of the obligation? She'd find a way.

'Mac and I are supposed to have dinner with Uncle George,' she said in dismay.

Tom stood very still for a moment. 'I thought we agreed to end this farce. So cancel it.'

'I can't,' began Jamie, ready to explain, but anger was flaring up in his eyes.

His voice was deadly. 'You can, but you're saying you won't.'

'If I have to put it in those terms, then I won't, but let me explain—you'll agree—'

But his anger was too fast and too hot for her. He was suddenly out the door, slamming it after him.

'Tom, wait—' she jerked it open and ran down the hall, but he was already out of the building and striding down the walk when she reached the front door. Wearily she turned back. There was no point in following him, she knew, because he would refuse to believe she had anything in mind but thwarting her uncle.

Wearily, she trudged back down the hall. When he calmed down she would explain—if he calmed down, if she had the chance, and if it was not too late by then.

CHAPTER NINE

THE next day Jamie listlessly cleaned her apartment and tried to sort out her emotions. Her mind reeled from hurt, anger, and a determination never again to let Tom Malcomb throw her into such turmoils of happiness and despair.

Love was too hard on the heart, she decided, and what she needed, if she ever decided to get involved with a man again, was someone comfortable, who could be a supportive companion—then she stopped that idea in mid-thought. She never wanted another man in her life.

She was going with Mac Lumas to have dinner with her uncle, and Tom Malcomb could go fly a kite! The next moment she was searching the telephone directory to find Mac's number and cancel the plans for the evening.

What am I doing? she wondered. How could any man, even Tom Malcomb, put her into such a tailspin? And she couldn't cancel out on Mac. She had blackmailed him into the situation, and now, if he could gain by it, she was obliged to give him the chance. Money and the security of a contract from Stone & Stone might be all that was needed to make him and his Susie lifelong honeymooners. She would just have to explain that to Tom.

Tom would understand. He was a person sensitive to the needs of others, he put a value on their own relationship, and would feel her obligations if he were in her position. All she had to do was tell him the entire story. *If* she could keep him still long enough to listen, she amended, thinking of his hasty departure the night before.

'Jamie Stone,' she glared at her reflection in the silver teapot she was dusting, 'you haven't got the brains God gave an animal cracker!' Hadn't she just made another rule about Tom Malcomb? Rules were made to be broken, but she was getting ridiculous. The reflection in the teapot was twisted, out of proportion because of the shape of the vessel. As twisted as her emotional life, she thought as she considered it. Amazing how straightforward her life had once been, and how entangled it had become.

'That's people for you,' she told the reflection. All her problems could not be laid at Tom's feet, she knew. Velma was wound up in them, Llewellyn and Hugh Belmont. Mac was responsible for her immediate worries—no, not *responsible*, she corrected herself. She was in her difficulties because she cared, cared for them and about them.

Even her position on the receiving platform had come about as a result of sympathising with those salesgirls she had watched in Phoenix. If she dumped all these new people out of her life, she could straighten both her life and that emotional reflection. But then where or what would she be? The girl from Arizona, she decided, the girl who had no idea what it meant to have a best friend. That wasn't what she wanted, and even if she did, there was no going back. Her heart had not come equipped with a reverse gear.

Jamie's morning and part of the afternoon were devoted to the chores of cleaning and grocery shopping. By four she was satisfied with her work and devoted the next two and a half hours to the care of her person, concentrating on her hair and hands. Work in the warehouse, she had discovered, was not conducive to natural glamour, and neither were household chores. Her hands had suffered most, and the repairs to her manicure made the night before had not lasted through the scouring and scrubbing of the morning.

'Another discovery on how the working girl lives,' she mused as she held up one hand, surveying the short nails she had been filing. She smiled as she remembered her reaction to Velma's nails that first day on the job. The naïveté of the non-worker! she thought. She knew her own looks had suffered as her time was taken up by the daily grind on the platform, taking care of herself, her clothes, and doing her own cooking and washing up. Fatigue and a refusal to let down her living standards had left facials and manicures low on her list of priorities.

Untroubled by the nervous indecision that had accompanied her date with Tom, she chose a light wool suit dress in smoke blue, brushed her dark hair into a long pageboy, and was ready when Mac arrived. She was slightly amused as his eyes travelled over her; his nod of appreciation was for her punctuality, and not for her looks. Definitely a man in love with another woman, she thought. Lucky Susie. As they walked out to the car, Jamie crossed her fingers behind her back, a childish action, but her desire to help Mac and Susie was bringing out a childlike enthusiasm in her. Something had to be gained out of the aching heart she was carrying about.

She might be childlike in her enthusiasm, but Mac was business-minded. As they drove out to her uncle's house in the west end, she fingered the crisp, cream manila folder that lay on the seat between them. She wondered if he truly understood what was required to impress a man like George Stone, but the evening wasn't too far advanced before he surprised her again.

The folder had been left in the car during dinner, but it only took Mac a moment to bring it in when the time was right. Even though the mood was temporarily broken when he left to get his information, his leaving the material in the car kept him from appearing too anxious.

While Jamie sat waiting with her uncle, George grinned at her across the ornate coffee service.

'I like your young man,' he said, holding out his cup again. Jamie had been aware of the speculation in his eyes when she and Mac exchanged a comment. Obviously he was assessing their every look to discover any loverlike symptoms. His relaxed mood came from the absence of them, Jamie knew. She was slightly bothered by her inability to put on an act, but she wasn't sure she could carry it off. Straightforward Mac would certainly botch his part!

She wondered if George would be so relaxed if he knew about the trouble between her and Tom. Despite all her self-assurances, she was unsure they could patch up the argument. There was only so much forgiveness in any person, she reasoned, and possibly she had pushed Tom past his limit. She was aware that she had botched it; the goal once shared by both Stones and both Malcombs might now be out of reach.

'I said I like your young man,' George repeated.

'Oh,' Jamie came out of her gloomy reverie. 'Obviously I do too.'

'Not terribly exciting,' added George, watching her furtively.

'Exciting enough at the right times,' Jamie countered. 'He's a man with the good sense to know when to turn on and when to turn it off. After all, he has a business to run and so do I.'

What a dull life that would be, with love filed alphabetically, she thought, but was rewarded by the consternation on George's face. There had really been no time for them to get to know each other well; obviously he was accepting her attitude as real. She wanted to laugh as she saw the worry crease his brow. Behind his dark eyes, sudden desperate thoughts were swimming like little fish. Jamie sat back, thinking the next move was his.

Let's see how he'll counter that, she thought.

Mac returned with his folder and Jamie forgot her battle of wits with her uncle. She listened to the big truckdriver make his bid for a contract. With her training she could see he was never going to make the grade in big business. He was too honest; he admitted his weak spots as well as his strong points, explaining that he wasn't 'biting off more than he could chew,' as he put it.

Still he had a good understanding of business as it pertained to him, and Jamie had nothing to blush for in the mental processes of the man she had blackmailed into being her escort.

At first, George was restless, and Mac, for all his hard work in preparing a prospectus, could not seem to interest him. Both Mac and Jamie were glum when George excused himself for a few minutes. But when he returned, he gave Mac all his attention, and at the end of the driver's spiel, virtually promised him the contract.

When the business was over, and the conversation turned to sports, Jamie left the two men arguing about their favourite football teams and strolled out into the yard. The house next door was the object of her going outside, though she only stood for a while and stared at it over the hedge. It had been her mother and father's home when she was born, and where she had lived until she was three. Twenty-one years had passed since she had lived there, so both the house and yard had changed a great deal, she thought. And as a three-year-old, she had probably never stood out in the moonlight gazing at it. Nothing jogged her memories, so she walked back in the living-room, to find the subject of sports exhausted and both men a little restless.

When she and Mac left the Stone house, Mac was, for him, loquacious.

'I'm going to see Mr Franklin next Thursday or
Friday,' he told her as if she hadn't heard the arrangements. 'I'll have to give Mr Stone a chance to speak to
him first.' Mac had forgotten that particular suggestion
had come from Jamie.

'You could take that contract to the bank and get the
loan for your truck,' Jamie suggested, enjoying his
excitement.

'Yeah, I could do that,' Mac agreed as if it too was a
new idea and not previously discussed. 'We ought to
celebrate—how about stopping off at Richie's?' At her
blank look he explained, 'It's a new place that has pretty
good music. I've been wanting to take Susie there—' he
hesitated but regained his exuberance. 'We should celebrate.'

'And then again with Susie when she comes back,'
Jamie reminded him.

'Sure,' he grinned. 'We'll celebrate setting the date.'

His remark left an empty space in Jamie. Suddenly she
was impatient with his happiness, and recognised the
envy in herself.

Turn to the flip side, she ordered her emotions. This
was a big night for Mac and she wasn't going to ruin it for
him.

New or old, all cocktail lounges seemed to be alike,
she thought, or at least they were in her experience.
There always seemed to be the same dimness, the music
was a bit too loud, and the odours of drink and cigarettes
mingled to give the places a uniformity of character. But
the moment they walked in the door, she recognised the
band as a professional group that could stir its listeners.
Her fingers were tapping against her purse as the waiter
led them to a table.

That was a tune she would like to dance to with Tom,
she mused as she took the chair Mac held for her. She
saw Tom's face illuminated as she thought of him and

wondered if she was losing her mind. But while she wondered, the face stayed where it was, at the next table.

'Well, good evening,' he said. Jamie stared at him. Not accustomed to illusions, she wasn't sure whether they talked or not. When Mac nodded and said 'Hello,' Jamie decided she was still reasonably sane. Even if she had thought him up, the term was nightmare, since Daphne was with him.

'H-hi,' she stammered. He must wonder at her behaviour, and she made an effort to explain away her gaucheness. 'The dimness threw me. I wasn't sure it was you, and accosting strange men . . .' she let the words hang.

'Yeah, I don't need to get in a fight tonight,' said Mac, the first attempted humour since she met him. 'I'm too happy to hit back.'

'Great things happening in your life?' asked Tom, leaning forward to be heard over the music. He slipped an arm around Daphne's shoulders, a movement that cut into Jamie with a knife.

'He just had a long talk with Uncle George,' she said, feeling the necessity of throwing out a barb, hoping to jar him into removing his arm from around his date's shoulders. Let him make what he would out of that!

The town must have thirty cocktail lounges, she thought. Why did they have to end up at this one? Behind them, someone at another table had spilled a drink, and the laughter over such a silly incident was giving Jamie a headache.

'Glad to see everyone represented,' said a familiar voice from behind Jamie, and she turned to see Velma standing with her hand on the arm of a stout little man two inches shorter than the bleached blonde. Jamie could see Velma had taken in the scene, immediately assessed it, and with her forthright mind, had decided to remedy the situation. The pricing supervisor waved away the maître d'.

'This is what I call luck,' said Velma. 'Just what we were looking for. We're celebrating, and for that we needed a party.'

'What are you celebrating?' asked Mac, moving his chair around and pulling another from an empty table.

'Number seven,' Velma said complacently as she took a seat and smiled up at her escort. 'I'll soon be Mrs Horace Coleman. I've changed my name more often than my mind. What's one more time?'

Plump Horace leaned across and winked at Tom. 'This is a time when it's not as important to be first as last.'

At Velma's subtle instigation, the two small tables were pushed together, and the six of them were together almost knee to knee. They were male-female around the circle. Tom was on Jamie's right and Mac on her left, and she was increasingly uncomfortable as her attention strayed to Tom and she nearly forgot Mac's presence.

The dimness, the restricted glow from the two lamps on the table, only seemed to illuminate Tom's features, causing his eyes to light up in reflection, bringing to prominence his strong face and his capable hands. In his dark suit his body faded into the dimness, giving her the feeling that he was hovering just in the background, all the pull of his masculine charm invisible and therefore irresistible.

But Tom was also feeling the strain, she decided. He was not nearly as relaxed as when he had first caught sight of her, and his attentions to Daphne seemed to have a preciseness of predetermined calculation. Was she imagining that? she wondered. Was she interpreting his actions according to what she wanted to believe? She made an effort to appear natural as she leaned forward, raising her voice to speak to Velma.

'Have you set the date?' she had to shout over the music.

Velma shook her head, causing a silver butterfly to quiver dangerously. 'We've got to get together on vacation schedules—so we can have a honeymoon,' she shouted back.

Suddenly staid, quiet Mac leaned forward, his face as bright as the lamps. 'We'll be setting the date next week,' he announced so everyone could hear. 'I just had a long talk with Mr Stone!'

Great galloping horsefeathers! thought Jamie. She held on to her glass of white wine as if it were a life-raft. Mac, caught in the throes of his personal excitement, had not given a thought to how his two admissions would sound.

Across the table, Velma had been taking a sip of her drink, and had swallowed a piece of ice. While Horace pounded her on the back, Jamie cut her eyes at Tom. He looked as if he had been kicked in the stomach.

She opened her mouth to explain Mac's remark, and then decided not to. The shock of seeing Tom with Daphne had left her shocked enough to bring on an emotional numbness. Then the unexpectedness of Velma's appearance further confused her. But she was adjusting to the surprises, and her resentment over the situation was steadily growing.

Darn it, even if Tom didn't understand, she had a very good reason to be with Mac. He needed her help, and she had put herself under an obligation that demanded she assist him. She was sure, from what Tom had told her, that Daphne needed no such assistance.

Jealousy and a sense of being misused was building inside her. She wanted to cry, she wanted to fight. Her pride won.

'Yes,' she said, taking a sip of her wine before continuing, 'Uncle George was far more co-operative than we expected.' Just at that moment the music stopped and her words seemed to hang in the dark and suddenly still air. She had only meant to give Tom another jolt, but the ring of her words seemed to have a certain finality. She wished she could bite them back.

Horace, obviously not aware of the situation, and with an elation as great as Mac's, enthusiastically shook Mac's hand. Tom, with a forced heartiness, did the same.

Jamie slowly twirled her wine glass, wondering how she was going to straighten out her newest problem, the result of opening her big mouth at the wrong time.

But the difficulty wasn't insurmountable, she decided. All she had to do was offer a toast. Two—the first to Velma and Horace, then one to Mac and Susie. That would be a perfect opportunity to explain how a talk with George Stone tied in with their future happiness.

Daphne beat her to it. Her simple words, 'May the sun shine forever on the happy couples,' was simple, sweet, and even worse, left no room for Jamie to get in her explanation.

As if he could no longer stand the atmosphere of lovers, Tom caught Daphne's arm and almost pulled her on to the dance floor as the band played a slow number.

Jamie watched them circle the floor with regret. Whoever came up with the expression 'sweet revenge' certainly didn't know what they were talking about, she thought. Then seeing Velma watching her from across the table, she tried to rearrange her expression into a reasonable facsimile of enjoyment.

Velma started to lean forward, but at that moment Mac decided he wanted to dance. Since he hadn't noticed the blonde's desire to speak, he was nearly as insistent as Tom had been. When he led Jamie on to the dance floor, his first words were no salve for her ego.

'I wish I could call Susie,' he muttered. 'I sure would like to tell her how things have turned out.'

Jamie's heart soared. Another opportunity for an explanation presented itself. This one she was *not* going to lose.

'You should,' she announced with decision. 'We'll excuse ourselves, at least for a bit, and you can call. We can always come back.' She was thinking of how she would word their excuse. 'Mac's got to call his fiancée and tell her the good news,' was what she intended to say.

'No,' Mac dashed cold water on her plan. 'Susie and her folks are driving up to visit her aunt. I don't know how to reach her before Monday.'

Oh—rats! Well, she would just have to think of something else. But that thought too went the way of all her good intentions. She and Mac were still dancing when she realised Tom and Daphne had left the floor. She turned her head and saw them at the table, where Tom helped Daphne with her wrap and shook Horace's hand.

Rats and more rats, Jamie thought. Why was the world intent on thwarting all her efforts at explaining? And worse, why did she seem to spend her life trying to explain? She made a mis-step and trod on Mac's foot. By the time the dance was over, she had mis-stepped again; he stepped on hers. It was that kind of evening, she decided as he guided her back to the table.

Velma and Horace had their heads together, and judging by the way they pulled apart, they were discussing the romantic situation. Further proof of their conversation was in Horace's unhappy expression. Jamie was struck by his look of helplessness, as if he could not understand why all the world wasn't as happy as he was.

Jamie took her seat and gazed across the small lamp at Velma. There was no point in evading the issue.

'Go ahead, say "I told you so."'

For a moment the brassy blonde was nonplussed. Her eyes flicked to Mac before she concentrated on the glass in front of her.

'I don't know what you mean,' said the pricing supervisor.

'You said if we played that stupid game, nothing but trouble would come out of it,' Jamie said. 'Now Daphne has Tom, Mac has his Susie, and I'm out in the cold.'

Both Velma and Horace stared at Mac as if he were something from out of space.

'Susie?' Velma choked and pointed a finger at the big truck driver. 'You mean when he sets the date it's not for you and him—'

'Not with me, no,' Jamie answered.

Next to her Mac shifted. She glanced over at the big truck driver and saw his face change as the implications of the earlier conversation dawned on him. Beneath his dark tan he paled; his face that could be seen above the beard was splotchy.

'But I didn't say—he didn't think—' For a fearful few seconds, Jamie thought the bearded giant was going to faint. 'M-Miss Stone, I'm sorry.' He pushed back his chair. 'Maybe I can catch him—tell him the truth—I thought he *knew* about Susie.'

'I'm the one to handle it,' said Jamie, wondering how she was going to do it. After all, she could have straightened out the misunderstanding in the beginning, but instead she had chosen to let Tom think what she had thought would upset him the worst. The fault was more hers than Mac's.

'Well, we'll just tell him the truth,' Velma said with decision. 'That shouldn't be any problem.'

'Try it,' Jamie said morosely. 'I don't know why, but all you have to do is plan to explain, and the *entire world* gets in the way. Go back to your celebration. Mac is going to take my sad face home so I don't ruin anything else tonight.'

As Mac drove along the quiet streets, Jamie silently abused herself for not being able to submerge her own problems and be happy for Velma's sake. But Velma would understand, she decided. Anyone who had been through six marriages knew what it was to be down. Considering the misery she had been suffering over one romance, she decided the pricing supervisor was a brave woman indeed.

'What I don't understand,' she said to Mac, causing him to start at the suddenness of her voice, 'was how, of all places in town, we ended up in the same night club with Tom and Daphne.'

'I didn't have any idea they were there,' said Mac. 'And I want you to know, I'll talk to Tom Malcomb on Monday,' he added. 'I've been thinking about what I said, and I can't think how I could have been so stupid. I just thought everyone knew about Susie.'

As Mac reassured her, Jamie caught the different sound in his voice. She had no idea what he was covering, but she could feel the hollowness in his words. He seemed to be saying one thing and thinking another. The back of her neck prickled as if some present not visually recognised was riding in the car with them.

'Mac, you're not telling me everything,' she accused. She was gambling and she knew it; she didn't know Mac well enough to judge his voice that accurately, but her shaft, drawn at a venture, hit a target. The big man shifted on the seat and gave her a hesitant glance.

'I'm telling you all I know, Miss Stone. The rest I'm just thinking, and I don't want to lay blame where it shouldn't be.'

'What are you thinking?' demanded Jamie, at once suspicious without knowing why.

'I could be wrong—' The misery that had been hers

was now transferred to him. In his acute discomfort he ran a red light. His eyes kept switching from the road to her face. 'If I'm wrong, and your uncle found out what I said—'

'Mac!' Jamie's voice held the authoritative threat of three generations. 'I own as much of the store as my uncle. Don't make me your enemy!

'It's just that your uncle said we should celebrate. He mentioned the place, but he probably didn't know—'

'He knew!' Jamie lashed out. 'That old buzzard knows everything!' But the pieces of the problem weren't fitting together properly. 'When did he make this suggestion for our happy evening?'

'When you went out in the yard.'

'Oh—I wonder how he knew where Tom would be—' Then she remembered that he had excused himself after dinner and when he returned he had been happy as a clam.

'You know what he did?' she demanded of Mac. 'He called Abel Malcomb to find out where Tom was! Those two old crooks are not only deceitful, they're spies!'

Mac nodded. 'Probably overheard Tom making a reservation,' he guessed. 'Miss Stone, you won't tell your uncle? I need that contract. I'm sure sorry I messed things up.'

Jamie reached over and gave his arm a consoling pat. 'Mac, they helped to create the foul-up, and they'll have to live with it. I told you they're set on getting Tom and me married. Well, with our help, they ruined that little plan, so they just outsmarted themselves.''

Jamie turned to look out on the dark street and blinked away the tears. She had thwarted their plan, but she was the one who would suffer for it.

CHAPTER TEN

FOR Jamie, Easter Sunday droned by in an agony. The day before she had worked at cleaning her apartment until she had nothing left to do. She refused an invitation from Uncle George, not daring to go into his company and let him see her long face.

Better to stay at home alone and mope, she thought. But loneliness drove her out of the apartment. Across the street, the doors of the large old church opened early. Jamie had never been a churchgoer, but she dressed quickly and was in time to sit through a well delivered sermon and listen to the choir sing selections from Handel's *Messiah*. Twice during the sermon and more often in the musical part of the service she raised her eyes heavenward in a silent apology for her wandering mind.

From her place near the rear of the church, the turning of every dark, well-shaped head caught her attention and at her heart, causing her to believe for a moment that she was looking at Tom.

None of them could be Tom, she told herself several times. Did he go to church? She had no idea, but if he did, he would probably attend one close to his home. And where was that? she wondered. Amazing how little she knew. There were so many details that did not come up in general conversation.

On the way out of the church, she made a decision. She would simply call him and blurt out the truth, as she had with her name.

That's me, a blurter, she thought. The description seemed to be apt if not flattering.

Not until she had dropped her handbag and hat on the table inside the door did she remember she had no idea how to reach him. The telephone directory was no help. But, she wondered, why should she expect it to be? Uncle George had an unlisted number, and so would the Malcombs.

Was she ready to submerge her pride and call Uncle George? She wouldn't have to tell him why she wanted Tom's number, he would know. Somehow the old devil would figure it out before she had finished voicing her request, she thought. But pride was the least important issue at stake. Tom was right, they could battle the two senior members of the firm later. First she had to straighten matters out with Tom.

She dialled. No answer.

Unable to stay in the apartment any longer, Jamie grabbed her handbag, leaving the hat where it lay. She would have lunch in a restaurant near by and then go for a walk in the park. She had locked the door and started down the hall when the ringing of the phone started. The rush back to the door, the fumble in her bag for the keys, and getting the door open seemed to take forever.

Wait, wait, don't hang up, she begged, aiming her mental plea both at Tom and Uncle George. The time must have stretched out for the caller to; she was halfway across the living-room when the ringing stopped.

She waited for a couple of minutes, but the phone stayed stubbornly silent. Then, with dragging feet, she left the apartment again.

Neither her lunch nor the walk in the park helped any. Around her happy families and couples only heightened her lonely feeling. She left the park and went to a movie and spent the rest of the afternoon sitting in the dark theatre, staring at the antics on the screen. Both the actors and the story lacked the power to reach through her misery.

Monday morning finally arrived, and she greeted it with relief. At least she would know where to find Tom. No matter how he took her explanation, she would be over the suspense. Either he would accept her story, or she could let got of her hope and get on with her misery, uninterrupted by bizarre plans for straightening out the misunderstanding.

At the warehouse, she was just hanging up her light jacket when Velma stuck her head in at the office door. The pricing supervisor was at work earlier than usual, and her rush to dress was apparent. One of her little bows was nearly falling out of her hair, and one bleached curl was askew.

'Did you see him yesterday?' she whispered. No need to say who.

Jamie, feeling unequal to speech, just shook her head.

'Damn!' Velma breathed. 'I walked with his secretary from the parking lot. She said he's going to be late.'

'He and Daphne will be married before I tell him the truth,' Jamie muttered.

'Don't *say* that!' Velma hissed, and crossed her fingers as if she were warding off the evil eye.

This morning Jamie was grateful for the usual Monday morning rush. She chased from one shipment to another, trying to stay out of the way of the drivers as she examined the shipments for the information necessary to her forms. She had no time for her depression. Work, it seemed, was an excellent balm for her pain.

She turned from recording a shipment and noticed the clock. Eleven-fifty. The morning had passed quickly. She wondered if Tom was on the Malcomb's platform and was just turning to look in that direction.

Her view of the door was blocked by his physical presence as he approached her. The thrill of seeing him was overweighed by his purposeful step and his tight jaw.

'I wonder if you can take a moment from your hectic schedule,' he asked harshly.

Jamie laid the clipboard down on the nearest carton, not caring if it ended up in the pricing section, or a branch store across the state.

'I've been wanting to talk to you,' she said, feeling breathless and stupid, now that she had the opportunity to air all her rehearsals.

'If that's true, you shouldn't have been so hard to locate,' he snapped.

The latter part of his remark was momentarily lost under his implication that she might not be telling the truth. After suffering all weekend, her sense of injustice welled up, filling the nooks and crannies of her mind. There was no room left for the humility she had planned.

'How dare you take that attitude to me!' she bristled. 'At least I had a good reason for what I did on Saturday night—if you were snuggled up with Daphne for an altruistic reason, let's *hear* it!'

Tom's chin went up in surprise. Clearly he had not expected a counter-attack. For a moment Jamie had him at a disadvantage, but before she could press her point, he looked past her. His expression darkened, his eyes narrowed.

'At least Daphne doesn't hang around the warehouse!' he snarled, and stalked off.

Jamie was caught with her mouth open, the words shaped and ready to blurt, but with no target. She was thrown off her emotional balance so abruptly, she physically staggered.

'Now, wait a minute!' she shouted after him, but he pushed past Freddy and a truck driver and disappeared into the Malcomb's warehouse.

'Miss Stone, I came early—'

Jamie swung around to see Mac standing behind her.

Her anger at the retreating Tom transferred itself immediately to the hapless truck driver.

'Why weren't you late?' she demanded. 'Of all the times for *you* to be early—' She broke off her tirade when she realised the shrillness in her voice had attracted the attention of all the drivers, Freddy and Carl, and even the notice of a police officer who was driving by.

'I thought I'd straighten—' Mac started to explain, but Jamie wasn't having any.

'Just unload,' she snapped. 'And the next time you come, wear a *mask*!'

Leaving poor Mac looking befuddled, she hurried across the platform and into the Malcomb's warehouse. At first she saw no sign of Tom among the jumble of cartons, drivers and receiving clerks. Then she spotted him approaching a group of people off to one side of the floor. She was too angry to notice the faces in the group, even those she should have recognised. Her whole attention was on Tom. She intercepted him as he circled around a large shipment.

'I want to talk to you!' she announced. Her voice was precise, clipped, and as formal as it was shrill. 'We're going to have this out right now!'

Tom stopped in his tracks. His head turned towards the group of men, but caught up as she was in her anger, their presence still meant nothing to her. After one quick look his jaw set and he turned back to her.

'All right, let's have it out!' he snarled back. He started towards her, his steps so deliberate and menacing that she shied away from his physical presence and took shelter behind a stack of boxes.

Tom was momentarily stopped by the cartons, but he didn't hesitate to shout over them. 'What was he doing over there?

From the relative shelter of her position, she shook

one already shaking finger at him. 'He's making a legitimate delivery, and I'm sick and tired of you jumping to conclusions!' She was jumping to one herself, she knew. If Mac had just stopped by, she would be forced to strangle him, just to prove to Tom that he wasn't invited.

'Likely story!' Tom retorted.

Jamie suddenly felt their behaviour had degenerated into that of two five-year-old children. If they were going to solve anything, they had to discuss it like reasonable adults. Then all efforts in that direction faded from her mind, as Daphne strolled around the corner of Tom's office.

'Far more likely than telling me *she's* making a delivery,' Jamie answered back, pointing at the woman. Daphne had come to an abrupt halt as Jamie's words rang out across the warehouse floor.

For a moment Daphne looked around as if she wanted to find her own shelter, then inspiration lit her face. 'I came to join Uncle Abel for lunch,' she announced to the platform at large.

Jamie came out of her anger and landed on her pride. What was she doing making such a fool of herself? There she stood in jeans and a shirt, grubby from her morning's work, and behaving like a shrew. Across the crowded expanse of concrete Daphne was suave, svelte, and even if her excuse was a blatant lie, she was gracious enough to offer it.

Then Jamie's attention dragged itself around to the group of men. She supposed, somewhere in the back of her mind, she had registered the fact that Uncle George and Abel Malcomb were in the company of several well-dressed business men. She knew who they were and why they were there; the week before, Tom had mentioned that a group would be touring the warehouses.

She had made a fool out of herself in front of a select audience, one she would have to live with. All the fight washed out of her, and unable to face anything else, she turned to flee back to the S. & S. warehouse. But as she started for the door, she saw Carl, Freddy, Mac, and four other truck drivers standing in the entrance.

Making an abrupt change in her direction, she headed down the hall that led into the back of the Malcomb's warehouse. Maybe Tom would have her arrested for trespassing. But that would be a relief—at least she wouldn't know her other cellmates.

She ignored the hurried footsteps that followed her. Just as she was approaching the elevators, Tom grabbed her arm and swung her around.

'We said we'd have it out, let's do it,' he demanded.

Jamie felt as if everything inside her was going to explode any moment. She couldn't go on with the battle.

'You let *go* of me!' she shouted, pushing him away.

Either Tom was off balance, or her desperation gave her more strength than she ordinarily had, for he staggered slightly and would have regained his balance, but he backed into some low boxes stacked neatly against the wall. As he tried to hold on to her arm with his right hand, his left swung out and up, trying to catch himself.

An ear-piercing alarm blasted over their heads and for a moment they were frozen, looking up. In an effort to brace himself, his flailing hand had gone under the protective covering for the fire alarm and rested on the large red button.

'Oh no—' Jamie muttered. She jerked her head around, staring at the open shaft. With a clang the automatic system reversed itself and picked up considerable speed.

'Oh, damn,' added Tom, looking up at the ceiling as if doom approached. 'The vault's open too—we've got to turn the power off!' But he seemed loath to turn and deliver the order. Slowly he backed down the corridor, his eyes never leaving the speeding chain and cable system that served as elevator for the automatic carrier. Jamie too stared at it.

In moments hundreds of carts, and thousands—no, millions of dollars in merchandise was going come down that shaft. Like people fleeing a disaster, they would be pushing one another in their haste. She turned and fled.

As she rounded the corner and came out on the Malcomb's platform the first people she saw were her uncle and Abel Malcomb. 'Get the power turned off!' she shouted. While they gaped at her she whirled towards the door leading into S. & S. Hugh was pushing his way through the crowd blocking his way.

'Get everybody!' Jamie yelled at him. 'False alarm! No fire, but get everybody to catch the carts.' The moment it took for her implication to sink in seemed endless to her, but Hugh was actually quick in his understanding. Even faster was Freddy, who turned and sprinted towards the pricing section.

Jamie turned back to help with the first tall carts that were rolling down the corridor. Until then she had not noticed that the floor sloped. No detail for fast orderly movement had been left out, apparently. The carts in the vanguard were marked *FURS* and instructions for their storage were stencilled on the canvas sides.

Jamie made a leap to stop the first one, and on the other side of the container, Daphne added her weight. Together they changed its direction, sending it rolling into a shuttle van that was mercifully empty.

From both sides, volunteers hurried to help. Soon Jamie and Daphne were just in the way of the stronger men who could move the carts faster and more expertly.

Jamie took a moment to look over at the woman she thought of as her rival. Daphne, seeing the look, shrugged.

'It goes against the grain to let anything happen to mink.'

A call from Tom interrupted Jamie's reply. 'Get that truck in the bay!' he shouted from the corridor, and Jamie turned to see he was looking at her. She looked out on the street to see a large S. & S. shuttle van, riding high on its springs as if empty or lightly loaded. It was in a position to back right in and catch the carts.

She repeated his order, passing it along to George and Abel, who were trying to direct the moving of the boxes on the platform and make space for the fleeing carts. When George nudged Abel and they exchanged looks, she wanted to throw something at them.

See, they're working together, the quick congratulatory look implied. She wanted to shout at them to get on with the instructions and leave the games for later, but they wasted no time in ordering the driver to action.

Moments later, the lights went off and the raucous noise of the fire alarm stopped. The carts continued to roll down the corridor and out on to the platform.

They pulled the wrong switch! Jamie thought wildly, but as Tom came strolling down the hall, dodging the rolling carts, his relieved expression told her she was wrong. Of course there would be many still in the corridor, rolling down the gentle slope, pulled by the force of gravity.

Jamie turned to look out over the platform. Over the clang of the fire bell she had not heard the arrival of the the large fire engines. Abel Malcomb stood off at one side, talking to the helmeted firemen.

After the blare had stopped the sounds of the crowd on the platform and the clink of metal as the carts bumped against each other were single, disconnected noises each surrounded and divided by a fraction of silence.

'Keep your grubby hands off—I trapped them,' Daphne's voice travelled clearly to where Jamie stood.

'Not all of them,' Velma argued back. 'I caught one cart of furs, and four of designer dresses.'

'Let's do some trading,' Daphne replied thoughtfully. 'How about another fur for two of . . .'

The rest of their playful argument was cut off by George Stone as he turned to the group of businessmen touring the warehouse.

'This demonstration, gentlemen, was brought to you by Malcomb's, showing what use our automatic systems can be in case of fire and disaster—'

'I don't believe it,' said Tom. Until he spoke, Jamie had not realised he was close to her.

'He should have been ringmaster in a circus,' she replied, listening to her uncle making his spiel as if periodically they created total havoc just to test the equipment.

She looked around and sighed. It was total havoc, she decided. The incoming shipments that had been on the platform when the alarm went off were scattered about, piled on each other as room had been made for the escaping carts. The rest of the afternoon would be needed just to straighten out the mess. No deliveries could be accepted and confusion would reign for a week.

She hardly hoped to find her own platform in better shape, because she had seen Freddy, Carl, and several of their people pushing the escapees into their section.

The buyers for both stores were going to be screaming; the branches would be phoning and complaining. Most of the freight companies would be decidedly unhappy.

But they would straighten it out, she knew. At the moment she was too happy to have Tom standing beside her. Together, they had brought about the wreck, and he was by her side as they caught their breath. She looked shyly up at him and he grinned back.

'We did something on our own,' he said quietly.

Jamie laughed, not at his joke, but out of pure exuberance. His smile had made all the mess worthwhile.

'Mr Malcomb, I think I caused a misunderstanding—'

They both looked around to see Mac, who was squeezing his way between two carts.

'Go away,' Jamie ordered. She raised two balled fists which looked small and ineffectual against the expanse of his huge chest. Mac grinned and beside Jamie, Tom choked on a laugh.

'As long as everything's okay,' said Mac, and disappeared between the carts again.

'I guess that goes for me too,' said Daphne. She had approached them from behind, and stood smiling as if their togetherness was her doing.

'Game's over, I think,' observed Tom as she turned away.

Abel Malcomb, followed by George Stone, was also working his way through the clutter.

'You came to have lunch with me,' Abel said to Daphne, his voice loud enough to be heard across the platform. 'I know a great place—'

'I don't want to hear about your hollandaise sauce,' George Stone interrupted, his voice threatening.

'Forget that chef of mine,' Abel ordered. 'I'm going somewhere where they make these great hot fudge cakes, and hamburgers—' Before he took Daphne's arm, his hands described something huge and guaranteed to ruin a diet.

'And onion rings,' muttered George as he followed the others along the platform. 'Those clowns of ours never make good onion rings . . .'

As the three walked off, Tom's arm slid around Jamie's waist. She turned to slide her arm around his neck. When her gaze met his, she felt as if she was dissolving in the light of his attention.

'I want to tell you about Mac,' she said breathlessly.

'You did tell me,' said Tom. 'You said in the beginning that he was engaged, but I forgot it. His saying he was setting the date after talking to George threw me until I thought it over on Sunday morning. Then I couldn't find you. I came over, I called, and then I decided you were out with him again. I think I must be the jealous type.'

'It's nice to be valued,' said Jamie. 'I give up, I know what you mean about fighting those sweet old devils over the wrong issues.'

Tom kissed her gently. 'They may be sorry they threw us together. If we can do this when we're fighting, just think of what we'd do co-operating.'

'They're in for a shock,' Jamie agreed.

'Just as soon as we get back from the honeymoon,' said Tom.

No business discussed on our honeymoon, Jamie wanted to say, but his lips demanded hers for a more pleasant reason.

Author **JOCELYN HALEY,**
also known by her fans as **SANDRA FIELD**
and **JAN MACLEAN,** now presents her
eighteenth compelling novel.

With the help of the enigmatic Bryce Sanderson,
Kate MacIntyre begins her search for the meaning behind
the nightmare that has haunted her since childhood.
Together they will unlock the past and forge a future.

Available at your favorite
retail outlet in NOVEMBER.

DREAM—02

You're invited to accept 4 books and a surprise gift Free!

Acceptance Card

Mail to: **Harlequin Reader Service®**

In the U.S.	In Canada
2504 West Southern Ave.	P.O. Box 2800, Postal Station A
Tempe, AZ 85282	5170 Yonge Street
	Willowdale, Ontario M2N 6J3

YES! Please send me 4 free Harlequin Romance® novels and my free surprise gift. Then send me 6 brand new novels every month as they come off the presses. Bill me at the low price of $1.65 each ($1.75 in Canada)—an 11% saving off the retail price. There are no shipping, handling or other hidden costs. There is no minimum number of books I must purchase. I can always return a shipment and cancel at any time. Even if I never buy another book from Harlequin, the 4 free novels and the surprise gift are mine to keep forever.   116 BPR-BPGE

Name	(PLEASE PRINT)

Address	Apt. No.

City	State/Prov.	Zip/Postal Code

This offer is limited to one order per household and not valid to present subscribers. Price is subject to change.   ACR-SUB-1

Experience the warmth of...

Harlequin Romance

**The original romance novels.
Best-sellers for more than 30 years.**

Delightful and intriguing love stories
by the world's foremost writers
of romance fiction.

Be whisked away to dazzling
international capitals...
or quaint European villages.
Experience the joys of falling in love...
for the first time, the best time!

Harlequin Romance

**A uniquely absorbing journey
into a world of superb romance reading.**

Wherever paperback books are sold, or through
Harlequin Reader Service

In the U.S.
2504 West Southern Avenue
Tempe, AZ 85282

In Canada
P.O. Box 2800, Postal Station A
5170 Yonge Street
Willowdale, Ontario M2N 6J3

**No one touches the heart of a woman
quite like Harlequin!**

R-111

You're invited to accept 4 books and a surprise gift Free!

Acceptance Card

Mail to: **Harlequin Reader Service®**

In the U.S.
2504 West Southern Ave.
Tempe, AZ 85282

In Canada
P.O. Box 2800, Postal Station A
5170 Yonge Street
Willowdale, Ontario M2N 6J3

YES! Please send me 4 free Harlequin Presents® novels and my free surprise gift. Then send me 8 brand new novels every month as they come off the presses. Bill me at the low price of $1.75 each ($1.95 in Canada)—an 11% saving off the retail price. There are no shipping, handling or other hidden costs. There is no minimum number of books I must purchase. I can always return a shipment and cancel at any time. Even if I never buy another book from Harlequin, the 4 free novels and the surprise gift are mine to keep forever.

108 BPP-BPGE

Name   (PLEASE PRINT)

Address   Apt. No.

City   State/Prov.   Zip/Postal Code

This offer is limited to one order per household and not valid to present subscribers. Price is subject to change.   ACP-SUB-1